BLURB

When Maisie Swenson takes over as manager at Florida's elite Oceanside hotel, she's thrilled to move on site with her Momma and their basset hound, Bingo. She expected by the job description to cater to the crazy whims of some of the richest people in America.

Make it snow in Florida--check. Helicopter wedding--check. Deliver a baby--check.

But what was never on her job resume was dealing with the murder of business mogul Norman Olsen. He's a huge figure in the gaming video business, but now it looks like he had some dangerous enemies – including his own wife and son.

When the murderer targets the hotel again. Maisie thought the worst of her worries was getting fired. But, as she uncovers clues, the murderer focuses on Maisie. Suddenly, it's personal.

BOOKED FOR MURDER

CEECEE JAMES

-For my family. You guys are the best. I'll say it in every book I write. <3

EPIGRAPH

-Books are one of the fuels of life-

CONTENTS

INTRODUCTION

Book one of the Oceanside Hotel Mysteries

CHAPTER 1

My name is Louisa May Marigold Swenson, Maisie for short. How in the world my parents got Maisie out of Louisa May or Marigold, I'll never know. It's always been my theory that Momma wanted to name me Maisie to begin with. But with a Grandma named Louisa May and a father whose favorite flower was of the many-petaled orange variety, she just had to sneak it in any old way she could.

Momma has called me Maisie for my whole life, only trotting out my full name when I was late for supper, or she'd discovered the cookie jar was empty, or the dog had been given a haircut—although to be fair, I was five at the time. Still, I can hear her voice ring out over the air, especially at twilight on a summer's eve.

And not just because it's a childhood memory. No, Momma lived with me, along with her basset hound, Bingo. That dog was something else. The story that Momma tried to spin was that she got him for my birthday—my thirty-fourth birthday, mind you. Momma expected me to go ga-ga over the floppy-eared pup like I was still in pigtails unwrapping gifts under the Christmas tree.

Well, I did go ga-ga. I can't lie. Who could resist a basset hound puppy with those giant crocodile feet to match dark brown eyes?

Bingo adores me. I'd love to say that's unique but, truth be told, he adores anyone with food. I've always said he'd betray our whole family for a French fry, which made Momma frown. Although he loved all people, the dog was especially bonded to Momma. I think half because she was always here with him and the other half because she kept a box of Nabisco vanilla wafers nearby that she insisted were to aid with her digestion. Kind of supported my theory, because I had a good feeling they help Bingo's digestion pretty well, too.

I'm originally from Angel Lake, a gorgeous little town in Tennessee, but I recently scored my dream job down here in Starke Springs, Florida as a manager at the Oceanside Hotel, complete with a complimentary suite on the bottom floor. It's only two blocks from the beach and near the most amazing amusement park. No, not the iconic one with ear hats. We have a squirrel on ours. That's just our thing, and we do treasure it.

Technically, I applied for the hotel manager's job and moved down here from Tennessee to look after Momma. I wouldn't tell her that, though. She's apt to pull out a darning needle and threaten to chase me with it. Not that she could chase very far, but I'd rather not get her riled up.

Momma believed I moved here for the job, and because I'm desperate for her help in finding a man. "Maisie, you keep going like you are, and you're going to be living in Spinsterville," she liked to warn me. Her not-so-subtle hints let me know she secretly felt like she's my last hope to find me a good match. I'm pretty sure she actually believes she's the one taking care of me.

Truth be told, I haven't been having a lot of luck in the man department, so I could use all the help I can get. Or not get. Some days, I am completely okay with living the single life. Other days are so lonely even Bingo's sad eyes can't capture what I feel inside.

Anyhow, they say the strangest things happen in hotels, and I'm here to say they're right.

IT WAS LUNCHTIME, and I headed through the lobby back to my suite. My stomach made a grumpy unladylike noise, as I pictured the meal Momma had prepared. She cooked the meanest roast beef, butternut squash, and French-cut green beans that you've ever seen. That was one of the many good things about moving in together.

Opening the door, I took a big sniff. Immediately, I started coughing. *Dear heavens, what was that smell?* Somewhere between a cross of hellfire and burnt broccoli.

"Momma?" I yelled. My mouth went dry to see smoke hanging in thick swirls near the ceiling. I rushed to open the sliding glass door. Grabbing a towel, I started waving. I could just imagine the newspaper heading now. "Firemen break into hotel to find General Manager has set her apartment on fire. "Momma? Where are you? Are you okay?"

3

First to greet me was Bingo, the basset. He meandered over, tongue lolling and tail wagging. He seemed fine with the putrid smell.

Momma walked in next, shuffling in slippers and a pink housecoat and carrying a bag of microwaved popcorn. She seemed fine as well, immediately making me concerned. Her brassy red hair—she called it strawberry blonde—came from the salon down the street by a hairdresser named Genessa. Momma liked to say that Genessa was a far better listener than her own daughter and would make her a grandma before I do. I never knew what Momma was saying with that statement; was she threatening to adopt Genessa and replace me? Or was it just digging at the fact that I didn't have a husband or even a prospect on the horizon yet?

Momma reached for a handful of popcorn from the bag and put a kernel in her mouth. Half the bag sported black scorch marks.

"What on earth is going on?" I started out patiently, still waving my towel. Momma was stubborn and if I acted too eager, she might clam up for good.

"I made myself a snack to eat while I watch my stories."

Stories was what Momma called her soaps. She'd done that since I was a little girl. Her eyes opened wide and innocent.

I didn't fall for it. "You're just eating popcorn? I thought you were making lunch?" My stomach rumbled to underline that thought.

"Darlin', I'm on a diet. Swimsuit season is coming up in just a few more weeks." She shuffled past me and into the living room, carrying her charred bag.

Bingo quickly followed when he realized the food had left the room. I followed them, confused.

"Why is the popcorn bag black?" I asked, almost scared to hear the answer.

"Well dear. It happened like this. I saw a lovely craft on Pinterest. Button tiles. The plan was to make a bunch for the hotel convention tomorrow. Earn me some pocket money. But something's wrong with your microwave." She sent me a dismissive wave. Apparently, the conversation was over, as she emphasized by tossing another piece of popcorn into her mouth, her eyes glued to the TV set.

I chewed my bottom lip and headed back into the kitchen. Visions of roast beef, gravy and potatoes evaporated before my eyes when I saw the disaster awaiting me. *How could one little woman accomplish so much?*

Dirty measuring cups and bowls towered in the sink. I felt something crunch under my foot and glanced to see sugar sprinkled like deranged fairy-dust. On the counter were two empty bottles of Elmer's Glue, bits of leaves and flowers, and one of her recipe cards. I picked it up and read the recipe, smiling a bit at the smudged fingerprint.

Homemade Fake-Acrylic Buttons.

I tried not to cry as I scanned the rest of the counter, which was filled with used spoons, dirty towels, and a frying pan. What did a pan have to do with buttons?

Yanking open the microwave, I let out a scream. Globs of glittery glue were stuck to the bottom, sides, and ceiling. What the heck had she done, baked the glue to lava-exploding temperatures and then tried covering up the hideous smell by burning microwaved popcorn? Like that's a better, less obvious smell?

I was more than a little worried. Momma was a character, but she generally didn't do things quite this nutty. I grabbed my cell and dialed my closest friend, Ruby.

I'd met Ruby in junior high, during those awkward years when braces and zits defined me. She'd traveled from Florida to Tennessee that year for a summer camp, and we'd hit it right off. We'd joined the camp's fast-pitch team and played baseball with the other camps in the area. The next few summers we continued to meet up. Even in high school, we managed to work together as camp counselors. And, I have to admit, I became a champion baseball pitcher, and was pretty proud of my speed and accuracy.

Ruby answered on the third ring. "Hey, lady. What's cooking?"

"Funny you should ask." I reached for a sponge to scrub out the microwave. "Right now, I'm cleaning Momma's attempt at making diamonds in the microwave."

Ruby clucked her tongue. "That bad, huh? What was she doing?"

"I think she may have had it in mind that she would be the great bling proprietor for the Comic Convention tomorrow." I scrubbed at a particularly stubborn black chunk. Was I going to need a chisel?

"Oh, that's funny. You should have taken her up on it." Then, hearing my frustrated huff, she quickly changed the subject. "Have you ever overseen anything like a Comic-Con before? Are you nervous?"

"No, and no." My phone vibrated softly, alerting me to a message. "Send some good thoughts my way, I'm going to need them. I'll talk to you later."

"You better believe it! I want to hear all about it!"

I pushed the end button and squinted to see the text on the screen.

Inside the little green bubble were the words—*What are you wearing?*

Normally that'd be offensive, or romantic, depending on who was sending it. Instead, I groaned. The text was from my boss, the owner of the Oceanside Hotel, Mr. Timothy Phillips. Despite the awkward wording, he was asking what I'd planned to wear to the convention tomorrow.

My hands flew over the keys. *—Not a costume.*

I stared back at the microwave and rolled my eyes. I was going to need to steam it or something. I set a bowl of water in and hit the timer, then walked into my room.

There was my pink dress suit, pressed and hanging in the closet. I had a shiver of doubt run down my spine, but shook it off. It was going to be a marvelous day, and I was going to kill it.

CHAPTER 2

I wasn't as confident the next morning. Nerves prickled my spine as I smoothed my hands over my dress suit and wondered if I'd stick out like a sore thumb today.

The night before I did a bit of searching on the internet to see what the expectations were about costumes. The pictures were bizarre. I saw costumes from Ursula in the Little Mermaid, to Jack from the Nightmare Before Christmas, and everything in between.

Taking a deep breath, I glanced around the lobby, all prepped for a big show, and tried to calm my nerves. I was printing some last minute requested brochures, when the sound of a paper jamming in the printer dragged my eyes downward. It was the second time in a matter of minutes. I squatted behind the counter and tried to yank the papers loose. The pages were good and stuck. Great, I was now in a tug-of war with a stupid—

"Good morning, Ms. Swenson," a deep male voice said.

I jumped and peeked out over the counter. Mr Phillips! Where on earth did he come from?

A younger man stood next to my boss and looked at me quizzically. My mouth went dry. Whereas my slightly overweight employer wore a polo shirt and shorts, the other man was impeccably dressed in a three-piece suit that clung to his arm muscles. His dark hair was parted to the side, and his green eyes twinkled with faint amusement. It was apparent he was from old money and high class. Definitely far out of my league.

I willed myself not to blush as I stood and brushed down the front of my skirt. No luck. Heat filled my cheeks. A blonde wisp escaped my bun and fell in front of my eyes.

"Hi there, Mr. Phillips," I said and casually tucked the hair behind my ear.

His beady eyes narrowed. "I'm on my way to a golf tournament and thought I'd stop by. You ready for the Comic-Con today?"

"Absolutely, sir." I straightened my back.

The other man lifted a thick eyebrow as his gaze bounced down to my knee. My cheeks filled with heat. *Do.Not.Blush.* I cleared my throat and continued, "The booths are all ready and are filling with vendors as we speak. It's going to be a great event, sir."

Mr. Phillips nodded. "I don't want anything running sloppy. Keep a close eye on things and make sure everything goes smoothly. The hotel has needed something like this for a while— youthful energy and a full conference area. It's definitely a direction we need to keep growing in."

I nodded, still distracted by the man in the suit. Why was he staring at my leg? He caught me noticing and the corner of his mouth quirked up. Annoyance bubbled inside of me.

Mr. Phillips seemed to notice the stare going on between his partner and me. He offered an explanation with a haphazard wave of his hand. "This is my brother, Jake."

Brother?

Jake thrust out his hand. "Very nice to meet you."

I shook it and tried to warm up. "Nice to meet you, as well. Are you in the hotel business as well?"

The younger man's gaze flicked to my face with a slight smile before turning his head toward the overhead chandelier. Two thousand hand-hewn crystals hung from that chandelier; the hotel's pride and joy. "No. I sold my part in this a long time ago."

"Jake is a sommelier for a nice, local restaurant," Mr. Phillips volunteered with a hint of pride.

Jake dipped his head in a humble acknowledgement as his brother clapped him on the back.

"Wow. That's very impressive," I coolly said, not wanting to gush too much after his sardonic stare earlier.

"So, you've got this, then?" Mr. Phillips asked one more time.

"Absolutely, sir. Nothing's going to go wrong. It's going to be amazing."

He slapped the counter in a quick beat and then nodded. "Let's head out then, Jake."

Jake raised his hand and followed him out.

I stooped back to the printer. My knee showed from under my dress and made me gasp in horror. It was completely covered in blue ink.

My stomach squeezed at the sight of the ink puddle that had leaked out on the floor. That darn hair fell back in front of my face and I reached to tuck it back.

The movement made me freeze. *Had I just put ink on my face too? Was that what Jake had been staring at?* With a quick glance at the time and a groan, I quickly mopped the ink with paper towels, and then headed back to my suite to clean up.

OKAY, take two.

Feeling red, scrubbed, and inkless, I headed back to the front desk. It was here that my expectations for the day shot out the window.

The line was already out the door, and Clarissa, the other hotel clerk, was stuttering while helping a guest. I could tell the crowd had shaken her.

Normally, we don't offer early morning check in, but that was one of the stipulations the convention had required before booking, and Mr. Phillips had agreed to it immediately.

"Where were you?" Clarissa hissed while passing a room key to the guest in front of her.

I looked at the crowd and swallowed.

My earlier research had prepared me somewhat. But, I hadn't expected the fact that they would already be in costume when they came to the front desk. I'd just assumed, since it was so early, the guests would be dressed in regular street clothes and, later, prepare in their rooms.

That was painfully obvious that wasn't the case. Cartoon characters, super heroes, people carrying swords or in full body makeup of brilliant greens and purples—one by one, they lined up in front of the counter.

I braced myself for a long day.

It was halfway through the morning when I realized I needed to relax before my perpetually arched brow created permanent wrinkles. I checked the computer to confirm the name of the male creature in front of me. I asked myself again how I was supposed to match names and IDs when most of them were wearing more makeup and formed foam facial appliqués than a horror movie monster?

"Is this your first stay with us, Mr. James?" I asked, keeping my strained voice as professional as I could. I was getting wiped out. Next to me, I could hear Clarissa's was getting scratchy.

"Yeah."

Behind him, the line grew with more superhero characters. The crowd looked a bit unruly at the longer than average wait. My stomach tightened. *Do not arch your brows. Calm, cool, and collected.*

"And your date of birth?" I asked, bringing up his reservation.

"It's on my license. Right under Caleb James."

"Yes, but your license doesn't have yellow cat eyes and ram horns." I used more strength than any Pilates session I had ever done to keep the sides of my lips from curling into a sarcastic grin.

"November 23, 1989. Can I have my room key now or do you want a blood sample too?"

The contempt was not unnoticed.

I penned the room number on the empty line below his name, placed the plastic keycard into the slot of the pamphlet, and slid it across the lacquered walnut desk to the fur covered fingers tapping out their impatience.

"Enjoy your stay at Oceanside Hotel." I gave him my sweetest smile.

He smirked before stomping off toward the elevators. The smile melted from my face as the circular doors spit out three more cape-wearing champions who tromped over to join the throng.

I sighed. *Only two hundred more guests to check in. It's going to be great!*

I hated it when my subconscious teased me.

———

THE ENTIRE DAY was filled with creatures from all manner of games and fandoms. Some I recognized as the speeding blue blurs from a video game or the plumbing duo who always tried to rescue the princess. Other costumes just left me more confused and questioning my sanity.

Momma, having let go of her dreams of selling hand-made trinkets to the costumed masses, had come out to visit just one time. She'd wandered up to the front desk and primly rested her hands on the counter. I heard her suck in her breath sharply at the view of a group of half-naked girls with a red "S" emblazoned on their chests. With a look of disdain on her face, she arched one of her penciled-in eyebrows. "Maisie, what kind of business are you running here?"

"It's the Comic-Con, Momma. I was telling you about it, remember?"

She turned to me with a blank look and blinked.

"It's supposed to be fun," I added, sliding yet another key across the counter to a guest.

Momma sniffed. "Not lady-like fun. Go get those girls some clothes to wear or you're gonna have yourself an outbreak of pneumonia."

Just then a centaur ran by. Momma stared for a second before adding, "Come to think of it, the boys could use some, too."

She stared again at the guests before giving me a disappointed expression as if I was contributing to some poor girl's downfall and trundled back to our suite.

Finally, the other front desk clerk, Sierra, came to relieve me. Sierra was not my favorite co-worker. Many moons ago, she'd applied for my position and had been denied. Understandably so, I thought she resented my presence. Her eyes narrowed at the sight of me.

"Sierra, can you take over for me? I need to check out the convention hall."

She nodded coolly, and I sighed. I wasn't sure how, but I'd try to mend that relationship later. At the moment I felt more tired than I'd been in ages, and was convinced each of my shoes weighed ten pounds.

I moved heavily across the foyer to take a quick peek into the convention center. Two of the six sets of double doors were propped open into a wide entrance and were nearly impassable with the mass of people moving in and out of the room.

The noise inside the enormous hall was deafening, with walls lined with screens flashing with animated advertisements for the different games being showcased. The next thing to hit my senses was the strong scent of body odor. I wrinkled my nose.

Earlier, I'd sent three of my staff to mill about in there and keep an eye on things. I searched the room for them, now.

A man dressed like Thor stopped me. "Nice costume," he said as his eyes quickly traveled from my heels up my pink Dior dress suit, pausing a moment at my chest. I fought the urge to cross my arms and opted for a frosty smile instead.

"Oh, really? And who do you think I am?" I asked, curious.

"Easy. Dr. Harleen Frances Quinzel, Ph.D., before she turns into Harley Quinn."

"Who?"

"The Joker's girlfriend."

I opened my mouth to correct him when a shout echoed through the foyer. Heads of all colors, sizes, and shapes swiveled to the center of the convention room.

That scream was flooded with panic. I half-ran in that direction. "Excuse me, excuse me." The repetitive command rolled off my tongue as I shoved past fur and brightly colored satin costumes, trying to reach the source of the noise.

"She's trying to kill me!" The scream was definitely a female, and her voice shushed the crowd. My ears buzzed at the sudden silence.

CHAPTER 3

*a*drenaline fueled my weaving through the crowd. Along with a strange claustrophobia. I had to fight my own instincts to kick and shove.

"Excuse ME!" I yelled. With one last nudge, I made it past the ring of spectators.

My mouth dropped. And that was saying a lot, considering how the day had been going. A young blonde woman wearing only a bit more than a bikini—there was a metallic band of ruffles circling her waist—stood with her fists clenched and face screwed into a snarl. Another young dark-haired woman stood in front of her dressed like an Amazon warrior, that is if Amazons had discovered fluorescent green paint. The dark-haired woman's black-lined eyes slitted with disdain at the ruffled bikini girl. While the costumes made the situation alarming at first, I soon recognized it as a boring old cat fight.

My eyes tried not to roll out of my head. "What seems to be the problem?" I stood as a referee between the women.

"SHE has been chatting with MY boyfriend and sending him pictures!"

Wow, really?

"He wrote to me first. Plus, I am wearing more in those pictures than you're wearing right now in front of hundreds of people."

"You know I'm Saturn Girl! We already talked about this. What are *you* supposed to be?"

They both looked like they were about fifteen years old. "Look, I'm going to have to ask you two to lower your voices and calm down, or I'll have to ask you to leave." I threw a little "teacher's tone" in my voice, hoping it would produce the results I needed.

The crowd mumbled and slowly moved away from me as they began to lose interest. Authority had arrived so the clothing and claws would stay in place.

At least, I hoped it would.

One man there appeared to be in his late fifties. He stood out to me because he wasn't wearing a costume. Instead, he had on a blue checkered shirt and khaki shorts. Sweat trickled down his face, his head firmly covered with a straw fedora.

"All right, ladies," I said, moving my hands in a calming fashion. One of the attendants I'd assigned to the room sidled up. Who's that guy again? Oh yeah, Gary Smith, the maintenance guy. He was a new employee like me. With a crowd this large we needed all the help we could get.

Apparently, he took his new role a bit too seriously. Right now, he was dressed in a business jacket and sunglasses. I half-expected a mic to be clipped to his shirt sleeve like an FBI agent.

The two young women watched me expectantly. That teacher tone worked better than I thought. "What's going on here? Do you know each other?"

The blonde flashed a guilty look at the Amazon woman. "Yeah, I guess so."

The Amazon woman shrugged her shoulders. "We've known each other since kindergarten."

I moved closer to them. "Well, what's going on then?"

The blonde sighed. "I just didn't like her getting into my business. Texting my boyfriend," she sent that last statement with a snarl.

"Ladies." This time it was the man with the hat that stepped forward. "No more fighting. What man is worth a friendship?" He smiled beseechingly at them.

"Yes, Uncle Norman," the blonde answered, glancing up at the brunette.

"Come here," her friend answered, reaching for a hug.

Well, that was easy.

Their uncle smiled and motioned with his hands toward a booth. "Go have fun, kids. No more fighting."

The young women rejoined the crowd. I studied the man, still sweating under the fedora. "Thank you for your help. Are you feeling okay? I know it's hot in here."

His smile was wide and genuine. "No, I'm fine. I'm always sweaty. Part of getting old, I guess." He glanced around the room. "You did a real nice job in here."

"Thank you. So, you're their uncle then?"

He laughed and stuck out a red hand. "That's just what they call me around these things. Name's Norman, Norman Olsen."

I shook it, keeping all reaction to his clammy palm from my face. "Nice to meet you. I'm Ms. Swenson. I'm the manager here. Are you staying at the hotel, Mr. Olsen?"

"I did book a room here, mostly for any of my employees that wanted a place to change. I live about twenty minutes away. In the Palisades."

My eyebrows flickered at the name of the exclusive housing development. Starter homes ran at ten million plus in that neighborhood.

"Well, it's nice to have you here at the convention. If there's anything you need, don't hesitate to ask."

"Thank you." He pulled out a toothpick from his front pocket. "Cinnamon," he said pointing it at me. "I'm trying to quit smoking."

Now that he mentioned it, I could smell the spiced scent. "It's not easy. I commend you."

He put it between his lips and moved it from side to side. "Old age. Keeps taking away from me all the things I love, and replaces them with things I hate. Like ear hair." His eyes twinkled at his own joke.

How on earth do I answer that? I opted for a wise smile.

"Anyway, like I said, you've done an excellent job here. I go to these all around the country."

"Oh, really? It's nice to know we compare."

"Yeah. I actually developed that game over there." He removed his toothpick and pointed it across the room to a screen flashing swords. "That's my baby."

My eyebrows raised, impressed. "You must love coming to these things and seeing the fans of the game then."

He looked around the room with a satisfied smile. "Nothing better in life than happy people." He slid the toothpick back in his mouth and spoke around it. "I see one of my associates, so I'm going to head over there. Thank you again for your help."

"No, thank *you*!" I answered with a small wave of my hand.

He drifted away until his fedora blended in with the many other headdresses in the crowd. I sighed and glanced around for my other employees working the convention. After making eye contact with Stan, the other maintenance worker, and receiving a thumbs-up in response, I squeezed my way back through the crowd.

It was a painful trek as more than one person stepped on my feet. Glad I wore my nice shoes, I thought sarcastically. Finally, I arrived at the front desk where Sierra flashed me another sour look.

"You're back," she stated.

I ignored the tone. "Just for a minute. I'm going to my room for lunch. You need anything, call me."

"You do what you need to do. But, if I was the manager, I wouldn't be taking a break right now." She sniffed.

"I've been out here since six. It's been eight hours, and I need to eat something. I'll be back shortly." I could feel her eyes blazing into my back as I marched down the hallway to my room.

As I unlocked the door, the sound of an avalanche of pans greeted me. Good grief. What problem waited for me now. I almost couldn't take another thing. I had to seriously consider if I wanted to continue inside.

Too late. Bingo heard the door open and raced baying around the corner, his big ears flapping.

"Hi, big boy," I whispered, sliding off my heels. I groaned at the soft feel of the carpet. Leaning down, I scratched behind the dog's ears before moving into the kitchen.

Momma was there, this time clad in an apron. She smiled at me, her red curls pulled back into a bouffant.

My mouth dropped open. Momma had very liberally been into the makeup, somehow emulating a cat eye complete with blue eyeshadow.

"You like it?" she asked, batting her eyes.

"Wow." I sat on a stool and stared. Don't hurt her feelings. "It's quite dramatic. How'd you learn to do that?"

"YouTube videos." She stepped around a pile of pots on the ground.

The suite had a lovely kitchen area with one tiny flaw. There was only one cupboard to store the pans. Even though I'd told Momma we needed to downsize, she still insisted on keeping every pot, pan, and broiler that she'd ever owned. So, they were stacked haphazardly in the cupboard like clowns in a circus car. And, every time she opened the door, nearly every pan fell out.

I shivered. Even though I loved Momma's cooking, I thought about pushing for us to eat takeout more often just to avoid the noise.

She passed me a glass of sweet tea and went back to whatever was bubbling on the stove. I took a long sip, the sugar coating my mouth and seeming to give me instant energy.

"YouTube videos, huh?" How was it that my mother was more technologically advanced than me?

"Yes. This wonderful gal named Miss Carman." Momma whisked at the tomato soup in the pot, then opened the oven to check on the parmesan covered garlic bread. "She says 'Flick with the eyeliner. Flick! Flick!' And, so I did." Momma closed her eyes so I could admire the said flick.

I took another drink and studied the makeup—Momma had always reminded me of Raquel Welch, and the eyeliner just accentuated that. "It's lovely, Momma."

She preened a bit as she went back to her whisking. In another moment, she had the bowls dished up and was slicing the bread.

I looked around the kitchen filled with warm sunshine. Peace started to seep into me as I relaxed. Bingo lay sprawled out in a rectangle on the ground. *This life... it's pretty, darn good.*

AFTER RESTING FOR A BIT, I felt fortified enough to get back to the job. I hated the sight of my shoes, and my feet throbbed a few times sadly as I slid them back on. I shoved my cell in my suit pocket and, after kissing Momma's cheek and giving Bingo a rub on the neck, I headed back to the front desk.

The foyer was still milling with people. I peeked into the convention room—crowded as expected—and noted none of my staff looking bored. Satisfied that everything was going as planned, I headed down the hall to the side of the building where the pool was located.

It was quiet back here. Ninety percent of the hotel's rooms were filled for the Comic-Con. What remaining guests we had were probably at the amusement park or the ocean, the two main attractions people came into the town of Starke Springs for.

As I walked into the pool's enclosure, I heard a loud clang coming from the chain link fence. I turned to look, but didn't see anything. Hedges from the dog park obscured the other side. *Must be a dog.*

There was one man in the water, floating by the pool's famous, yellow water slides. The man bobbed slowly in an inflatable chair, and I just had a quick glimpse of a cigarette in his mouth before he had his back to me.

This was clearly a no smoking area, as marked by several signs. "Sir?" I called.

He didn't move. Of course, he would ignore me. Impatience flamed in my chest as I realized I was going to have to walk around the entire pool to get his attention. Heaven help him, if he turned his back on me again when I got to the other side.

I stepped cautiously along the pool deck, noting the huge puddle of water on one side. Terrific. Was it leaking? Finally, I made my way around.

"Sir?" I tried again. "You can't smoke here."

He stared at me through thick sunglasses, not moving a feature. I frowned. Something was off. He was a little too still.

"Sir?" A flicker of alarm grew in my chest.

I studied the item in his mouth and nearly gagged. It wasn't a cigarette. It was a slender rectangular package.

And his face wasn't blue from makeup.

TEN MINUTES LATER, the ambulances had arrived, bringing a crowd from the convention hall following the stretcher to the pool. After dialing 911, I'd tracked down Mr. Phillips on the golf course, and he was also on his way.

As the emergency workers pulled the man to the edge of the pool, a crowd began to form. Mouths of centaurs, superheroes, and villains hung open.

"Back! Everyone back!" Two police officers commanded as they walked down the line and herded the crowd outside the pool's gate.

I whipped my cell from my pocket again and called my maintenance crew to get them to come help corral the guests back into the hotel.

As I hung up, the police were pulling the body from the water. One officer retrieved the item from his mouth and placed it in a clear bag. He murmured something that sounded like, "Granola bar," to his partner.

I looked away, frowning. Immediately, the crowd grew restless with loud comments.

"What happened? Is Uncle Norman dead?" A voice from the crowd immediately set off a chain of questions being fired from every direction.

"Dude, is *that* Uncle Norman?"

"Uh, I don't know."

"Man, you're right!"

"Ah, man."

I watched one guest pull out his phone to take pictures and stalked over there.

"Everyone inside! Please! Right now!" I shouted to be heard over their conversations. Luckily, my maintenance men arrived.

They both walked up to me. "You doing okay?" Gary asked, his hands jammed in his business jacket pockets.

"Not really.

"What do you want us to do?"

"I need you guys to get everyone back inside, if you can."

He nodded and they both headed to the crowd. Together, along with the officers, they began to turn the human tide back inside the building.

Glancing at the scene, I was relieved to see two of the officers holding up sheets to prevent the onlookers from taking further pictures and videos.

I followed the crowd back into the hallway. "Keep going! All the way to the foyer, please. The police are handling things. Please, be considerate of the friends and family and wait until they make a statement...." I shook my head.

The crowd had stopped moving. They weren't listening. My jaw clenched. I hated not being heard.

One young man closest to me looked like he was about to cry. "Dude, he was like family. He's always supported his fans. He responds to all the tweets and posts and everything. This sucks." More and more faces appeared distraught.

"I'm so sorry." I told the young man with a ball of pity in my gut.

"He's a legend. He really cares about his games but cares even more about the players and his fans. He was an awesome guy. I wonder what happened."

I wondered the same. Tears began to flow down the many faces around me, leaving clean tracks through the blue, purple and green face paint. The poor man had hundreds of fans, and they seriously cared about him.

My cell phone vibrated with a text. My stomach sank like I'd swallowed a brick as I read it.

CHAPTER 4

My boss was not happy with me, which he expressed succinctly with his text message—*I thought you said you could handle things.*

I didn't see how I could be blamed. We had signs at the pool stating there was no lifeguard, and the man was not in good health. I saw with my own eyes how he'd been sweating, and he'd apparently been eating a granola bar when he died.

Mr. Phillips arrived approximately thirty minutes after the coroner left. He hemmed and hawed, and did a lot of scowling, while I followed his pacing, waiting to be addressed with something other than his first blustered comment of, "How could this have happened?"

Finally, he left for the evening with the demand that I be up early to make sure the second day went off without a hitch.

Because the show must go on, and one accidental death wasn't going to stop it.

THE NEXT MORNING, I awoke to yet another text from my boss
—*Take flowers to Mrs. Olsen. Extend our sympathies.*

The flower arrangement was waiting for me at the front desk. It
was beautiful. I fluffed up the baby's breath around the vibrant
oranges of the tiger lilies, blues from the bird of paradise, and
pinks and whites of the hibiscus flowers, all colors that seemed
such an odd contrast to the grim event for which they had been
ordered for.

Leaning in to smell a lily, I steeled myself to confront the poor
woman. I was not looking forward to the awkward exchange.

*I'm so sorry we found your dead husband floating in our pool. We aren't
going to charge you for the room that your husband will never return to
and here are some lovely flowers.*

My throat tightened at the thought. Good heavens. Honestly,
what would the woman say to that?

At the foot of the counter was a leather suitcase. After the
police had pilfered through Mr. Olsen's room for evidence,
housekeeping had come along and packed it up. I glanced at the
suitcase and closed my eyes. There was a note, along with the
code to the front gate. I was to transport it back to her house.
Hopefully, the flowers would act as a buffer.

Who was I kidding? The idea of even interrupting her mourning
was a horrible thought. What if she broke down crying? I'd
never been very good at that stuff and already felt about as
helpful as a hangnail.

I sighed. Well, come what may, it was up to me to return the items to the widow.

I had the house number and plugged it into my phone's GPS. Laughter coming from the convention room jangled my nerves as I typed. Today was the last day of Comic-Con, and the sounds emanating from the convention room seemed almost vulgar.

I couldn't understand it. A man was found dead, and these people were still enjoying their fantasy worlds. He was supposed to be their hero. Then again, I guess it made some sense to escape from the reality of death to a world where you got a do-over if you died.

Address routed, I slung my purse over my shoulder. After a little finagling, I hefted the vase in my arm and gripped the suitcase handle in my other hand. I took a few steps before I realized the arrangement nearly blocked out my view of what was ahead of me, and tried to peek around the flowers.

Standing in front of me was Jake Phillips. I gasped and abruptly stopped, causing my ankle to slightly turn as the suitcase bumped into my heel.

Jake lifted an eyebrow in that arrogant way I was already getting to know so well. "Ms. Swenson," he said with a slow dip of his chin.

"Oh. Hello, Mr. Phillips." Baby's breath tickled my nose. I resisted the urge to blow it away and instead cleared my throat and tried to look dignified. "I'm just on my way out to deliver these to Mrs. Olsen."

He glanced at the luggage and then the huge bouquet. "Do you need a hand?" His dark eyes looked mysterious with those words. He gave a tiny smile.

I swallowed. I was unprepared for how that smile affected me. Sank right into my belly and stirred up butterflies. *What's the matter with me?* "No, I think I have this. Thank you." As fast as I could, I marched out the door.

The revolving door took a moment to navigate. My cheeks flushed as the suitcase jammed in the doorway, causing the door to stop. I pushed the door to free the luggage and pulled the case in after me, clutching the flowers like an oversized piñata. I swear I could feel his eyes on me. I couldn't help a quick glance and shivered with embarrassment. A corner of his mouth was turned up in amusement.

I couldn't even throw a confident smile back. The flowers nearly filled my mouth in the tiny space. With mincing steps, I waltzed the door around until it spit me out on the other side. Shaking my hair off my shoulders, I gripped the suitcase and walked to the parking lot with confident steps.

My little car wasn't much, but at least I didn't have a car payment. I threw the suitcase in the trunk, with a belated thought that I needed to treat it with more respect, and then packed the flowers on the passenger seat floor. With a sigh, I slid into the driver's seat and once again examined the GPS map.

THE DRIVE to the house was uneventful. I punched the code into the wrought iron gate and held my breath as it swung open.

This was my first time in this neighborhood. Everything about it screamed luxury. The cars in the driveways, the paved bricks on the road, the gorgeous trees and landscaping.

And the houses, my mouth hung open at the expansive porticos, the white pillars, stonework and bargeboard on the gables.

Mrs. Olsen's house was similarly spectacular. I pulled into the driveway and took a deep breath. Other than my car, there was just one other parked near the garage. That seemed odd. Where are the people comforting the grieving widow? Family and friends? Perhaps there were more vehicles parked inside the garage.

At the front door, I bit my lip. *It's now or never, girl.* I balanced the vase against my hip and rapped hard on the door. The flowers seemed to grow heavier as I listened for footsteps.

There was a rustle of movement and the mumblings of at least two voices before the sounds of someone approaching. The door opened, revealing a young woman.

"Yes?" she asked, her eyes quickly taking in my face and the flowers in my hand.

"I have something for Mrs. Olsen."

She opened the door wider. "I'm Mrs. Olsen."

My mouth almost dropped open. Luckily, I caught it in the nick of time. I'd been expecting a housekeeper and was caught off guard at her response. I was also slightly stunned at how beautiful she was. In my mind, I'd pictured a woman in a flowered shirt and wide, sensible sandals in her late fifties, with red, puffy eyes, not this tanned blonde woman in fitted slacks and a peach-colored silk blouse. After all, Mr. Olsen had been balding and at least eighty pounds overweight. Not to mention appearing at least twenty years older than the woman before me now.

She tucked a lock of hair around her ear and smiled, her eyes startling me with their brilliant shade of blue. *Colored contacts maybe?*

"Hello, there," she breathed. She glanced at my hands, and I remembered why I was there.

I straightened. "Mrs. Olsen. On behalf of the Oceanside Hotel, we wanted to personally express our condolences." My head dipped in my best expression of sadness. "And I'm here to return ..." I paused. Would she start crying at my next words? "Your husband's effects." I lightly tapped the handle of the suitcase to draw her eyes down.

"Oh," her face went blank. Tears seemed to magnify her eyes, and she blinked hard.

A lump rose in my throat. "Again, I'm so sorry."

She raised her chin and lifted her arms, seemingly unsure if she should take the flowers or grab the suitcase.

"Where would you like them?" I grabbed the handle of the suitcase.

"Please," she sniffed and took a step back, "just set them on the side table over there. Thank you."

"I'm sorry to bother you, and I know this isn't much of a consolation in this difficult time." *Did I seriously just call her husband's death 'difficult?'* I held the flowers in front of my face so she couldn't see the heat I felt in my cheeks. The suitcase wheels caught on the lip of the threshold and nearly caused me to trip forward, before riding smoothly on the wood floor.

"They're very beautiful," she said, standing back against the wall as if she wanted nothing to do with either of the items in my hand.

Moving carefully to the table, I finally was able to safely set the heavy vase on the dark lacquered wood. I slid it away from the edge and braced myself to maintain a neutral face before turning back toward the widow.

"If there is anything else I can do for you, please just let me know." I couldn't help but scan for the other voice. Surely if she had a visitor, they would be in the sitting area. It must be someone who didn't want to be seen dealing with their grief.

A wall of family portraits caught my eye. On a shelf above them sat a flag in a triangle display case. I quickly glanced away, but not before one of the pictures caught my attention.

Mrs. Olsen cleared her throat. "I appreciate the sentiments, as well as the floral arrangement. I do not, in any way, place blame for my husband's demise on the hotel. So please, there is no need to spend so much time and effort on appeasing me."

I blinked at her words. I hadn't considered that she would put the hotel at fault. Why would she?

CHAPTER 5

*W*hy on earth did Mrs. Olsen mention that about blaming the hotel? The man likely had a heart attack.* The questions swirled around in my head all the way home. I was in a near panic when I parked. Suddenly, my job performance wasn't looking so good. Someone dies at the first event I oversee, and now there's mention of "hotel" and "blame" in the same sentence. It didn't matter that she said she wasn't going to do it. Those declarations could turn on a dime with a word from the right attorney.

Chills ran down my spine at the thought of lawyers.

As I walked back toward the hotel entrance, a bright flutter of color caught my eye. Yellow by the pool. What was going on now? I stalked over there, my heels digging into the grass, and peered through the fence.

Three plainclothes policemen were there, along with Gary, the maintenance guy. Gary fiddled at his baseball cap as he watched the officers.

"Is there something I can help you with?" I called out, feeling slightly powerless on the wrong side of the chain link fence. The gate was locked on this side, with the only other entrance being through the hotel.

The officers glanced indifferently at me and then proceeded to ignore me. My eyebrows raised, and I shoved my shoulders back. I tried a different tactic. "Gary!"

His head jerked in my direction. My tone must have gotten to him because he came over quickly.

"What's going on?" I whispered. More like hissed. My fingers curled through the chain link. I hated feeling helpless and ignored.

"The police are suspecting foul play," he murmured.

Fear hit me like a bucket of cold water. "What? Last night, they said it was a heart attack?" The idea was frightening coming so soon after Mrs. Olsen's declaration.

Gary pulled off his baseball cap and ran his hand over his sweaty head. He puffed out his cheeks. "They're saying now that they're going to drain the pool."

"Drain the pool?" My mouth went dry. This was the worse news I could receive. What was a hotel without its pool? I thought this investigation was over and done with, an open and shut case. I had customers who specifically booked this hotel for its well-known serpentine slides. "Why on earth would they do that?"

I studied the police again. Two male officers were conversing by one of the drains. A female officer continued to stretch more yellow caution tape.

It was obvious the police weren't going to acknowledge me. I needed to get in there. Spinning around, I quickly made my stab-walk way back to the front door.

Sierra was at the front desk and gave me a frosty look as I entered. "Took you long enough," she said.

"Did you know the police were out at the pool?"

She looked at her nails. "Mmmhmmm."

I gritted my teeth to keep from snapping back. "And you didn't think to call me?"

Arching an eyebrow, she gave me a smirk. "It's your job to know. You're *supposed* to be in control around here."

I knew Sierra wouldn't forgive me for taking her job, but would she actually sabotage my job? I didn't have time for this and marched down the hall and out into the pool area.

One of the officers looked at me as I approached.

"Hi," I said, with my hand out. Police shake hands, right? The officer walked over with a cool glance at my hand. Okay then. I dropped it and continued on. "I'm Ms. Swenson, the manager here. Is the investigation still going on? I was told last night it was pretty cut and dried."

The female officer glanced over at the sound of my name. She hurried over. "I've got this, Vic," she said, addressing her partner. He gave me another unreadable look and walked back to the edge of the pool.

"Maisie?" she asked, slightly hesitant. Surprise filled me at the use of my first name, and I studied her. She was taller than my five and a half feet. Hard to see her hair and eye color under her hat and glasses, but it looked like a shade of brown.

"Yes?" I answered, feeling a hint of trepidation.

"I'm Detective Kristi Bentley. Ruby's sister?"

My mouth dropped open. Kristi Bentley? The last time I'd seen her, she was only twelve years old. The Bentley parents had a messy divorce, and she left to live with her dad while Ruby had stayed back with her mom.

"Oh, my gosh!" I exclaimed as surprise and joy joined the chaos of emotions tumbling inside. Plus a weird reassurance. I felt like I finally had someone in my corner, for the first time. "It's been so long!"

She smiled, pleased to be recognized. I knew in the other circumstances we would have hugged, but here we had to stay in our professional roles.

"So, Detective Miller," she pointed to the officer she'd called Vic, "will be conducting interviews with anyone still at the convention that attended last night. We'd like to request use of one of the meeting rooms to question the possible witnesses and determine who may have known the victim."

I couldn't help shivering at the word, *victim*. "I'm completely shocked. How do you know he was ..." I swallowed hard, "a victim?"

"Unconfirmed at this point. But people don't usually die with granola bars in their throats."

"Oh, my." Her words brought a vivid picture, and the pool area spun around me.

"You feeling okay? Need to sit down?" she asked.

The air chilled my skin even though I knew the temperature was well into the upper eighties. I shook my head and tried to calm my queasy stomach.

"So, you're going to drain the pool?" I asked, steering the question back into topics I could handle.

Her brows knotted in confusion. "No. Where did you hear that?"

My gaze darted to Gary, which she followed. With a sigh, she leaned in closer to me. "I need to tell you, that guy hasn't been very helpful."

"No?" I was surprised. Gary was fairly slow, but usually very dependable.

"No." Her voice held no room for doubt. "I thought we were going to have to threaten him with hampering an investigation. Maybe you could talk to him and tell him to cooperate with us?"

I nodded. He probably was trying to protect the welfare of the hotel's main selling feature—the pool with its two famous slides —but we definitely didn't need more bad press here.

"As far as your question goes, no, we aren't draining the pool. We did find something interesting." She glanced at her partner to be sure he was busy then whispered, "We found the victim's wedding ring at the bottom of the pool."

"Are you sure it's his? It could be anyone's. We clean the pool every night and find all sorts of things."

Her eyebrows rose with certainty. "Yep, his wife mentioned it was missing and described it to a T. But that's hush-hush, so keep it to yourself."

I nodded.

She clapped me on my shoulder. "We'll be in touch."

I WALKED BACK INDOORS FEELING numb. The first big event that was completely on my shoulders now involved a murder. Sierra scowled at me again from the desk as I walked right past her.

I needed a moment to clear my thoughts.

Bingo greeted me as I stumbled like a zombie into the suite. I walked over to my desk and slumped into the chair.

My computer stared at me, waiting to be brought back to life.

"You working on one of your stories?" Momma called. After a minute, she came through the archway carrying a glass of iced tea. "I brought you something to drink."

I accepted it and raised it for a sip. A lipstick mark marred the edge of the glass.

"Looks like you took a mouthful, Momma."

She shrugged. "I nursed you with these puppies right here." Momma pointed to her still bountiful chest. "You can share a drink with your mother."

My eyes fluttered closed, not needing to ever be reminded again of my nursing experiences. I took a gulp of the iced tea, as I tried to process the latest events.

"They think it's murder, Momma."

Momma harrumphed and crossed her arms over her paisley silk bathrobe. "I saw those policemen running around down there when I took Bingo out. You think it's true?"

"I don't know. I think I'm in shock still. I was just talking to him not an hour before." The cold chill returned.

"Probably his wife."

"My stars! Why would you say that?"

"It's always the wife. She probably has another man or wants some money or something along those lines. You know how folks get with money."

I watched as Momma eased herself into the chair adjacent from me. Bingo padded after her and flopped between the two of us. I smiled as his big brown eyes rolled up to look at me. We got lucky to have such a sweetie pie. Always a spot of joy no matter how crazy the day.

Sighing, I turned my laptop on, and after opening the browser, typed in Norman Olsen's name.

Momma watched with curiosity. "So, you going to check out his Instagram? Oh! You should check hers! There will be something there, I'm sure." She winked.

I snorted. Momma should just do this for me. She knew her way around the web better than I did.

"Alright, let's see what we can find out about him." I scrolled through the Google hits.

"Well, that's weird. Apparently, there was a recent dangerous threat to Mr. Olsen's company." I read further. "Olsen Studios shut down over a possible bomb threat. Police are searching for the suspect." My brow furrowed. "I wonder if they ever found him? I don't think the law takes kindly to bomb threats."

"It's today's video games, I'm telling you. What do they expect? You make a world for people to learn to enjoy violence and they'll start being violent in the real-world. Serves them right. Not like those good old fashioned games we had. When I was a child, we played Piggy in the Middle."

"It doesn't serve anyone right. That's not nice." I shook my head as I continued to scroll.

Momma watched me, and her brows creased with concern. "Now, don't you go making me worried. It's the police's job to find the killer. I was just watching on Cold Case where some young woman got involved in what she shouldn't have. They found her years later, and do you know where? In a suitcase, that's where." She waved her finger at the laptop and gave me a knowing look. "Just because you write mysteries, doesn't mean you should go around looking to get involved in them. You aren't Nancy Drew."

"I know, Momma. But this time it involves me. And Mr. Phillips isn't happy." I frowned as I thought of Sierra breathing down my neck for my job.

"Well, you didn't kill him. Why would it cause you any grief?"

"It still happened during an event that I was the manager over. I don't need the beginning of my career to wear the badge of 'And it all started with a murder.'"

"Pish!"

"Plus, we're kind of booked up for the next few months. The last thing I need is a slew of cancellations or even having the police lingering around next week. This mess needs to be cleaned up. The sooner, the better."

Momma leaned back in the chair, frown lines bristling from her lips like whiskers. I knew that expression. She was not happy.

"Come here, Bingo." She patted her lap, and the dog wandered over.

"Momma, he's not a lap dog. It's not good for him to jump."

"Well, how can I pet him then?"

"Bend over and pet him."

She sniffed. Peeked to see if I was watching, then she pulled out a vanilla wafer from her pocket. I rolled my eyes as she gave it to him discreetly. As if I didn't see. She already had him trained in being spoiled rotten.

I typed a bit more, searching into Norman Olsen's past.

Most articles were about his new game coming out, the one he was at the Comic-Con to showcase. It was some adventure and fantasy game, with mythological creatures and people using magic. Although his game and company had faced many setbacks, the game seemed to be widely anticipated. His fans were thrilled and talked about him as if he was some kind of king of the gaming world.

And then, just as I was about to give up finding anything new, the next link took me by surprise.

CHAPTER 6

*T*he new link was a shocker.

It was a picture of one of my recent hotel guests and Mr. Olsen. And I recognized which one it was, Caleb James. The one with the yellow cat eyes and ram horns who'd given me a hard time yesterday. In the picture, he was dressed in his cosplay outfit and holding a sword to Mr. Olsen's throat. The company's owner had his hands up in mock fear.

Underneath the photo, it said, "Mr. Olsen welcomes his favorite fan and biggest competitor."

That wasn't too unusual? Was it? I knew Mr. Olsen had fans. The sword at the neck was just a coincidence.

But, biggest competitor ... what exactly did that mean? Caleb was just a kid, twenty-four if I remembered his driver's license correctly. How did a kid become a conglomerate giant's competition?

I took another sip of tea, noting the ice was nearly gone. I wiped the condensation from my hands onto my skirt and looked for more info, but that was it. Just the short blurb along with the picture.

Outside, I heard someone yell, "Aww, come on." I stood up and pulled the curtains back from the window. The police had left, and Gary was shaking his head at a guest standing on the other side of the fence, obviously telling him that the pool was off limits.

This case had to get solved before wind of the pool's closure made it out to the general population. As if a death wasn't enough to dissuade guests ... I could see it now, reservations plummet, and Mr. Phillips continued to blame me. Momma, Bingo, and I are out on the street.

I shook my head as a vision of Bingo with a red handkerchief holding all of his belongings tied around his neck flipped through my mind. No, this case had to move faster.

"I'll be right back, Momma," I said.

Resting back in the chair, Momma had closed her eyes.

I got up quietly to leave.

"Where are you going?" she asked, her eyes abruptly opening.

"I'll be back for dinner. I thought you were sleeping."

"Pish," she said. "I was just checking my eyelids for pinholes."

I smiled as I left the suite and walked down to the front desk. As I neared the foyer, my steps began to feel weighted. *Should I really be getting involved?*

50

But, heck, I was the manager here. It would make sense that I would check on my guests since, technically, their stay here was affected by the death of Mr. Olsen.

At the counter, Sierra played with her cell phone, her feet propped up and the same sour expression on her face.

"How's it going?" I asked, moving over to one of the computers. Quickly, I searched to see if Mr. James had checked out yet.

"You know," Sierra said, not making eye contact, "I wouldn't get too comfortable around here. This should have never happened."

"It's not my fault someone died." I tried to keep my tone even. "This occurs all the time in the hotel industry."

"Not died. Murdered." At that, she plopped her feet down from the counter and turned toward me. "It never would have happened if I was in charge. I would have hired more security."

I ignored her. More security might have helped. But Mr. Phillips had given me a strict budget, and I'd been determined to make the convention happen under that amount, hoping I'd make a good impression.

Well, it made an impression all right.

Caleb James showed up as still checked in at room 307. I glanced at my watch. Nearly noon. Caleb could still be sleeping for all I knew. I closed the computer window to avoid the prying eyes of Ms. Snoopypants next to me, and grabbed my notebook and pen.

Just as I was about to walk away, I noticed something. Slashing down on Sierra's bicep to her elbow was a puckered, red scar

Catching me looking, Sierra blushed and yanked on her shirt sleeve, swiveling on the seat until her back was to me. I blinked hard. The scar was so long and gnarly, it kind of took my breath away. *Come to think of it, Sierra always wore long sleeves, even on the hottest day.*

Shaking my head, I hurried for the elevator. *I have too much on my plate to worry about that, now.*

Arriving at the third floor, I headed down to the economy rooms. Despite the term, the rooms were rather nice, just the typical two queen beds and a bathroom setup. Room 307 was on my left.

Swallowing the last of my hesitations, I firmly knocked on the door and then stood in view of the peephole with my hands clasped behind my back. What was I going to say? Inquiries into the murder seemed a bit out of my job description, but would this kid know?

After a few seconds of shuffling, I heard a tired-sounding, "Yeah?"

"Mr. James, it's the hotel manager, Maisie Swenson."

His muffled movement was punctuated with the snap of the door being opened only as far as the slider lock at the top could allow.

"What do you want?" One eye glared through the narrow gap, below a mop of messy black hair.

Ah, the rudeness of youth. Or was something else going on?

"I was wondering if I could talk with you for a moment about Mr. Olsen?" I kept my voice soft and as non-threatening as possible.

"Why?" The door shut a centimeter.

"The police are talking to everyone, but there are a lot of guests at the event, so they asked some of the staff to help them out." I was happy I had my notebook. It helped the impromptu excuse look more legitimate.

"Right now?" The closing door hesitated.

"Is now a good time?" I decided to use my trump card. "If not, I could just write you down on the list...."

His eyes narrowed. "Yeah, alright. Hold on."

Caleb shut the door and disengaged the lock before finally opening it wide enough to invite me in. My nerves zinged as I stepped over the threshold. If he was involved, I could be making a very big mistake by walking into his hotel room without anyone knowing precisely where I had gone. Shrugging off the apprehension, I walked in and headed over to one of the two chairs at the round table near the window on the back wall.

"Do you mind if I sit?" I asked.

"Help yourself." He crossed his arms over a rumpled t-shirt that looked like it had been slept in. "So, what you wanna know?"

He looked so different without the yellow contacts, horns, and claws. So ... normal. I studied him further. Actually, he looked sad and tired. The tension left my body as he slumped into a chair opposite of me.

"I'm just going to jump right into this." As I wrote down his name and hotel room number at the top of the pad, I noticed a few tennis rackets and clear, plastic tubes of balls in the corner. The gear was black and fluorescent green and marked with the emblem of an expensive sporting good company. "You play tennis?"

"Look, can you just get to the point?" He crossed his legs, one knee poking out through a tear.

"Okay. Did you know Mr. Olsen?"

He cocked his head, scanning my face.

"Sure. Anyone that plays computer games does."

"Did you know him outside of the gaming world?" I tried to keep my breathing even and my tone casual as I doodled on the pad.

He sighed. The silence grew between us. I gripped the pencil tighter, determined not to make eye contact. *Just give him some time.*

Finally, he uncrossed his legs with a thump and leaned forward. I hazarded a quick glance. His head was in his hands, his fingers making his hair stand on end. He let out a long groan, and then mumbled out, "The police are going to find out sooner or later, but yeah. He's my dad."

My mouth dropped open. I'd thought maybe an employee, or that he worked for the competition ... but dad?

He looked up then, his eyes rimmed in red.

My heart squeezed. The grief I'd expected to see with Mrs. Olsen, I was seeing right here.

"Mr. James ... Caleb. I'm so sorry, I had no clue." The breath felt sucked out of my lungs. Here I was thinking I could sort something out, and instead I stomped all over someone's most painful time.

He sighed again and sat up, his hair sticking out in all different directions. The light from the window fell across his face, sharply defining it in half. "It's fine. We weren't really close, and I don't exactly get along with my step-mother."

I wanted to reach out, to touch him, give him a hug even, but it felt too awkward.

He shrugged and looked back. "Is there anything else?"

I licked my bottom lip and glanced at my notebook, not sure how to proceed next. Maybe I should see if he wanted to stay another night free of charge? I opened my mouth to ask the question when the room's door beeped and swung open.

CHAPTER 7

A young woman walked into the suite, wearing a short white skirt and tennis shoes. Behind her was a similarly dressed man.

"So, what do you have to teach me in here?" she laughed as her fingers trailed down his arm.

Caleb cleared his throat.

Both the man and woman jumped with surprised expressions. The young man shrugged off her hand with a nervous grin. "Just let me grab some rackets." He walked over with a curious look at Caleb and picked up the two rackets leaning against the wall. He hesitated a moment as if he was going to ask something, his eyes nervously darting toward me. Bouncing the rackets against his leg, he stared at his friend for a second, and then said, "I'm just going to give Miss Cooper a lesson. You still up for that thing later?"

Caleb gave him a quick nod.

Okay then.

"All right, buddy. See you then." He nodded at me and turned back to the girl at the door. Gathering her waist with his arm, he ushered her out and pulled the door closed behind him.

"Who was that?" I asked.

Caleb rolled his eyes. "Look, you said you had questions for me. I've answered them. Are we done now?"

Part of me wanted to say yes, we're done. After all, I was intruding in every bad way all over his grief. But, at the same time, I was picking up on all sorts of warning flags. The room was rented for a single occupant, but that guy had a key. I couldn't leave without knowing who he was.

"Yeah, sure," I said, picking up my notebook. I tapped my pen against it a few times. "But I really need to know who that was."

"A friend, okay?"

"He had your room key."

"Yeah? So?" He crossed his arms with his brows lowered.

"Mr. James, I just need to know why an unregistered guest is staying at the hotel. That's it. It's no big deal."

He looked at me then, and his lip curled in a slow smirk. "You're the manager here, and you don't know who he is? What kind of horse and pony show is this anyway? I'm done here." He jerked his head toward the door.

His words, along with the smug expression he gave me stung a bit. It was as if I'd plummeted in his esteem. *Who was he to judge me? And why?*

Calm down. He's grieving the loss of his dad.

I stood up and held out my hand. "Thank you for your time. On behalf of the Oceanside Hotel, if there is anything I can do to help you, please let me know."

He glanced at my hand like it was a dead rodent and I thought for a moment he was going to spurn the offer. But slowly, he took it and gave it a brief shake.

Shoulders back, I walked confidently to the door, even though my insides quaked at how the interview had turned out.

The way he'd looked at me as if I should recognize the second guy ... what was it that I didn't know?

PONDERING THAT, I headed back down to my suite. Momma was asleep in front of the TV, her feet up on the recliner. One slipper had fallen off, and her foot looked cold. I smiled and grabbed the afghan off the couch and tucked it around her.

Such a precious woman. I'd moved here to rescue Momma from the rotting trailer she'd been living in after she lost the house that she and Dad owned their entire lives. Dad had been sick so long ... the medical bills ate up what was needed to pay for taxes. I'd found out too late that they'd refinanced, hoping to recoup some of the money. The loan had a balloon payment that was due the year after Daddy had died.

Life. You spent all of it trying to make a home, only to have it taken away at the worst possible moment.

She was with me now, and I was determined to make her golden years as happy as possible. Momma loved it here at the hotel. The staff adored her and kept her in the loop of all the gossip. She had her dog, her stories, and a microwave to create disasters. I had to make this work.

I sat at my computer and saw the Word document I was working on at the bottom waiting for me to work on it. I clicked to open the folder, and the title of my story jumped out at me. *The Clock Strikes Twice.* I scrolled to the bottom where the last thing I wrote was labeled "Chapter Eight."

The cursor blinked at me, waiting, almost mocking me as if saying, "What? No words today?"

Momma snorted in her sleep. I reached into my drawer for one of my peppermints and stuck one in my mouth. So many theories. I could totally put them in here. Sucking on the candy, I started to type.

The widow stared down at the coffin. A small smile played on her lips, but she wasn't worried about being seen because of the black veil that covered her face. She looked at the grave attendant and spoke quietly. "Shut the lid."

An hour and twenty minutes later, I finally looked up, feeling flushed from the creative journey. *There. Finished.* I reread the words and smiled. Right now, they felt like good words. I knew that the next time I read them, those same words would betray me and turn themselves into pedantic gobbledygook. I'd feel like the worst writer ever, but for now, they were magic.

Bingo nudged my leg and jerked me from my introspection.

"Hey, big guy. You want to go for a walk?" I reached down to scratch his neck. The Basset swung his heavy head up at me and blinked droopy eyes. Then he waddled to the door.

I tiptoed past Momma, who giggled in her sleep. *Okay, then, funny lady.*

I grabbed the leash and clicked it on Bingo's collar, and we left by the sliding door.

Bingo held his head high in new-found enthusiasm as we walked along the patio and around the hotel path. I was surprised to see the sun had sunk so low on the horizon. We followed the path down to a sidewalk that led to the "Park for Pups" area. Bingo was already speeding up in anticipation of the dog park.

My eyes were drawn to a large hedge to the left that covered the view of the pool. From that direction came the subtle splashes of someone taking an early evening swim.

Wait a minute. Someone was in the pool? Did that mean the police had cleared it?

I parted one of the bushes and peered through the fence.

Jake Phillips was climbing out of the pool by the ladder. He stepped over the yellow tape and grabbed a plastic bottle to take a drink.

Of course. His brother owned the hotel, so he probably thought he was above the law. The spinsterish-teacher feeling gripped me hard, and I almost stomped over there shaking my finger with a loud harrumph. Then he turned in my direction, and I ducked out of sight. *Nice going. So professional. Way to be a peeping Tom.*

I shook my head and softly clicked my tongue to Bingo, who had been patiently waiting at my feet with his tongue lolling out, and we continued along the path.

Reaching the dog area, I opened the gate, followed Bingo through, and closed it behind me. Once inside, I removed Bingo's leash. He was off immediately, trotting back and forth to catch the plethora of scents permeating the grassy space. I glanced at my watch. We had just about an hour until the evening sprinklers came on.

My eyes followed the basset hound as my brain wandered back to my conversation with Caleb. Something about him niggled at my subconscious. What was it? And who was the man who'd come into the room?

The more I thought about it, the more it bothered me. Why had it seemed the two men had exchanged guilty glances? And what was the story behind Caleb, anyway? He could afford to come to the Comic-Con and buy costume supplies and all the games, but he sure didn't dress as if he had a lot of money himself. Did his dad pay for this trip? How were they competitors? The picture on Google sure didn't seem like there was any bad blood between the father and son. But it was odd that it didn't label their relationship.

And maybe the biggest question of all, who inherited the successful developer's wealth?

Suddenly, my mouth dropped open. I remembered the picture on the wall when I'd brought Mrs. Olsen the flowers. That was it! Caleb was in it, only he'd looked awfully angry.

"Are you speaking with your dog telepathically?"

I let out a very girly squeal as my body jumped at the sudden male voice. I turned to the gate and saw Jake leaning on his forearms, watching Bingo. His dark hair was damp and his muscular chest bare. The towel wrapped around his waist left little to the imagination. I knew he was wearing swimming trunks, but I couldn't help the blush that rushed into my cheeks.

He raised his eyebrows. "I'm sorry, I didn't mean to scare you."

"I was lost in thought. I guess I've been a bit jumpy with all the excitement lately."

"That's understandable."

"Yes." Crossing my arms, I turned and focused on the dog. Where was Bingo anyway? "Was there something you needed?"

"Oh, no, I was just taking a swim while all the young, rowdy folk were still crowded into the conference." He brushed his hair back and forth with his hand to dry it.

"I'm confused … is the pool open? I know it had been closed earlier and saw the yellow tape."

He winked at me. "I won't tell if you won't." Then he pointed out into the park. "It looks like your little furry friend's found something."

Just then Bingo trotted up with something hanging out of his mouth.

"Bingo, what you got, boy?" I winced at the high pitch of my voice. Jake was going to think I was one of the weird people that used baby talk with animals. And since when did I care what he thought?

I walked over to Bingo and crouched down. Gently, I reached into his mouth for whatever it was he had found. *Please don't be a dead mouse. Please don't be a dead mouse.* As I started to pull it out, I couldn't help my noise of surprise.

CHAPTER 8

"Bingo! Let it go." An apprehensive feeling curled in my chest as I continued to remove the slobbery object hidden by the dog's flappy jowls. Relief flooded me at the feel of something metallic. A necklace or bracelet maybe?

"So, what does he have?" Jake asked from the fence.

"I don't know." I finally freed it from the dog and stood to untangle it. It *was* a bracelet—one of the medical alert types. I turned it over to read the name. The gray dusk light made it hard to see. "It's some kind of jewelry."

I brought it to the fence to show Jake. He took it from me and examined the links.

"Looks like the clasp snapped in half." He held it up to show me.

The clasp was broken, twisted almost beyond recognition.

Jake whistled. "The kind of force it must have taken to do that must have been huge. These bracelets are heavy duty." He lightly tossed it in the air and then handed it back over to me.

"I guess I better take this to the front desk in case someone's looking for it." I rolled my eyes. "Wow. That sounded about as obvious as asking if there were gumdrops in a candy store." My eyes widened. Yep. I just blurted that last sentence out loud because inward Maisie thought it would be funny.

I smiled and straightened my shoulders, trying to recover. The corners of Jake's lips lifted slowly into the first big smile I'd ever seen him make.

Well. Two points for inward Maisie.

I coaxed Bingo out of the park and sidled past Jake. He'd barely stepped back from the gate, and I passed through a scented cloud of chlorine.

For the first time in a long time, a man had me tongue-tied. Usually, I was the one who was in control, catching men off guard as they approached me. But this time, the tide had definitely turned.

I lifted my hand in goodbye and continued down the path, determined not to look back to see if he was watching. We meandered around the corner with me allowing Bingo to take his time.

It was just as I was pushing open the sliding glass door of my own suite that a thought occurred to me. *What was he doing swimming out there? Was he looking for something?* I glanced at the bracelet in my hand. *Was he looking for this?*

"Took you long enough," Momma called. She had her apron on again and her red hair tied back in a handkerchief. I slid the bracelet into my pocket and unlatched Bingo's leash. He immediately rambled over to Momma, who held a vanilla wafer in a trembling hand.

"What have you been up to, Momma?" I sniffed the air. Nothing burned. "You have a good nap?"

"Yes, and now I'm getting ready to make my special potato salad." She had a gleam in her eye as she announced this. She knew that I, along with everyone else who'd had a bite of that salad, had been after her secret recipe for years. "So, you should just get along now." She made a shooing gesture with her hands. "Scat."

Kicked out of my own home. Whatever. The potato salad would be worth it. I walked over and kissed her on her forehead, and she made motions like she wasn't about to take it before gripping me hard around the waist. "I do love you," she mumbled into my arm. "But don't be thinking you can sweet-talk me out of my recipe."

"You better not take it to the grave with you," I warned, as I left the kitchen in search of my heels.

She followed me out. "Fiddlesticks. I'll do what I want."

Finding them, I slid my feet out of my sneakers and tried not to whimper as I stepped into my work shoes. "Whatever, Momma. I'll be back in a bit. Don't burn the place down."

Momma's mouth fell open in mock surprise. "Girl! I'd never dare sass my mother the way you do!" She harrumphed some more and disappeared back into the kitchen. Two seconds later, the sound of clashing pans echoed through the suite, and a stray bowl rolled through the kitchen entryway.

"You okay?" I called.

"You just get on out of here now. I'm fine. I've been cooking since before you were old enough to suck a lollipop. Shoo!"

The last "shoo" got me, and I scooted out of the suite. You never knew with Momma. She used to threaten to come after me with a sewing needle, and she might just do that now.

The hotel hallway was quiet as most of the guests were out for their dinner. Interestingly enough though, as I neared the front desk, I could hear the convention still going live and strong.

This time Clarissa was working the desk.

"Hi, Clarissa. How's everything going tonight?"

"Oh, you're just in the nick time." She swiveled on her stool toward me. "We've had some noise complaints—two actually— about room 418."

"Have you sent anyone up there to check it out?"

She shook her head and flicked one of her blonde tresses over her shoulder. "I just got off the phone with the latest complainant."

I sighed. "Okay, I'm headed up there."

HALFWAY DOWN THE fourth floor hallway, I could already hear the yelling. *Lovely.* I hated these domestic disturbance types of calls. I plastered on my most no-nonsense face and gave two hard knocks on room 418's door. The noise I made was loud enough to halt someone in the middle of a rather colorful phrase of words.

At the break in the yelling, I called out, "It's Ms. Swenson with the hotel. Can you please open the door?"

"Great, now look what you've done." A male voice grumbled.

"Excuse me," I continued when the door remained closed. "I'll be forced to use my room key if I need to, but I'd rather have you invite me in. There have been complaints."

"This is so your fault." Anger threaded through a female's voice which moved closer to the door.

Good. They're taking me seriously. I stepped back. As the hotel door opened, I couldn't say I was surprised that the source of the trouble involved two familiar faces—the same scantily clad girls who'd been fighting in the conference hall a few days before.

It was the same woman who'd been dressed like an Amazon at the door. I remembered they'd said they were friends so I could understand them booking a room together. However, seeing the anger etched in lines around the young woman's face at the door did beg the question: With friends like this, who needs enemies?

She stared at me, one hand on her hip, the other holding the door half-shut to prevent a view of the room. "What? Sorry we were being loud. It was just a disagreement."

"We've had several complaints. How about you let me in so I can make sure no one is hurt."

She flinched. "Whatever." She turned and walked back in the room, leaving the door open.

As I followed her, my eyes were immediately drawn to a young man standing by the window. His arms were crossed, and he was glaring at the floor. The blonde-haired young woman was sitting cross-legged on one of the beds. She had a pile of crumpled tissues in her lap and was furiously squeezing another tissue into a ball with her hand, sniffling occasionally. There was a tall, clear bottle of vodka on the small table.

"Ok, I know the two of you are under 21, and I am assuming he is, as well. Is this the only alcohol you have in here?" I walked to the table and picked up the bottle, wondering how they obtained it.

"Yeah," the boy mumbled.

"I'm taking this unless you'd like the police to come get it."

"Just take it! And tell him to leave! He should go down to the pool and drown himself, just like he did that poor man!" the blonde yelled angrily.

My entire body froze. *Did I hear that right?*

The young man started protesting loudly, "What are you talking about? Are you crazy?"

In an instant, all three were shouting again. I tried to shake off the shock.

"Hey. HEY!" I yelled. Their screams trailed off as they looked at me. "You need to stop the screaming right now, or the police will be coming. I'm sure none of you would pass a breathalyzer test."

The Amazon sat on the end of the other bed. Her eyes focused on the boy at the window.

"Ok," I continued, catching my breath. "Accusing someone of murder is a pretty big step. Why don't one of you tell me what this is all about."

"My girlfriend wants to break up with me because she thinks I'm cheating on her with this wench." The young man pointed to the teary blonde and then to the Amazon brunette.

"Names please. Real names." Weariness descended on me. More drama.

"Her name is Danielle," His lip curled in disgust at the dark-haired girl. "And she's just trying to start trouble because she lost her chance to play mistress to that pervy old bas—"

"Whoa! Whoa, whoa." I held my hands out, knowing my eyes had to be bugging out. I turned to the blonde-haired girl. "What's your name?"

"Cynthia," she answered amidst sniffles. "And the truth is Andy really is cheating on me. He probably did kill that man!"

"Oh for—!" Andy burst out cursing.

"Knock it off!" I yelled, feeling at the end of my rope. I pulled out my phone. "If you don't behave yourselves and answer my questions, *I* will call the police. And I'll have you know I'm good friends with one of the detectives." The silence was immediate. "You," I pointed to the dark-haired woman who'd answered the door. "Name and tell me what's going on."

"Danielle. Cynthia thinks Andy's cheating on her because he and I have been texting a little bit. Just ideas about our cosplay costumes," she ended hurriedly. She glared at her friend. "So, she tried to get me back by spreading the rumor that I was hanging out with Uncle Norman—you know, the guy who died. I don't put up with that kind of crap."

"Is there any truth to the rumor?" I asked Cynthia.

Her mouth twisted to the side as she thought. "Well, Norman is —uh, was—known for buying presents and stuff. He liked to hang around us. All of us."

I felt queasy. Norman Olsen suddenly sounded very slimy. "So why would you accuse your boyfriend of murder?"

She glanced at him and then down at the twisted pile of tissues in her lap. "That wasn't nice. I was just mad. I don't want to lose him." Her lip trembled as she looked over at him. I wasn't sure she would be able to form more words, but finally, they tumbled out in a gasp. "I don't want to lose you, Andy. Not to her. Not to my best friend."

Andy didn't budge from his hundred-yard stare at the carpet. "I never did anything wrong. It was Danielle that sent the pictures. She's the one that was flirting with me."

Danielle rolled her eyes and flopped backward on the bed. "Please make this drama stop!"

I was with her on that one.

"Do you have anything to add, Danielle?" I asked, feeling like I was stuck on the set of a bad high school movie.

"You want to throw me under the bus, Andy? Fine." Danielle sat up with a steely glint in her eye. She turned to me. "I'll tell you why Cynthia thought Andy could have killed Uncle Norman." She crossed her arms across her chest. "Because Andy recently got fired from Olsen Studios."

Andy's eyes held something dangerous as he watched Cynthia that chilled my blood. Getting fired could definitely fuel hatred. But, was it enough of a motive to kill the man?

After getting the young adults to promise to keep it down in the future, I headed out of the room with the bottle of liquor under my arm. I didn't have much faith in their vows. I only hoped they would make it through the night without having the police called.

I felt bone-weary as I headed down the stairs to the suite. Somehow when I'd applied for this job, I never anticipated the creative route the job description would take. All I needed now was some dinner and my soft bed.

And maybe Bingo for some basset hound snores.

CHAPTER 9

*C*heckout day. I couldn't describe the relief I felt this morning. Today, all the guests would be gone from the Comic-Con, and maybe I could get back to establishing some sort of decorum and order around here. Dead bodies and investigations tended to disrupt that.

I left Momma eating a bowl of steel cut oats to go walk Bingo, who'd been scratching at the sliding door. It was early enough that the grass was still damp from the morning dew. The air smelled crisp, and Bingo's tail wagged in pleasure at being outdoors.

Inside the doggy park, I bumped into a female guest who was walking her tiny shih tzu. I left Bingo on the leash until the two dogs made their introductions. When they finished sniffing each other, I unlatched Bingo and watched him walk the park with his nose along the ground, even though he'd just sniffed the entire park the night before.

I heard the familiar tap-tap-tap of a ball bouncing on the tennis court. *Someone's getting their morning exercise.* I felt a tiny bit jealous, wishing I had a partner. Somehow, I couldn't imagine Momma would enjoy it too much.

Or move too fast, for the record.

I tried to watch, not getting a very clear view through the bushes. Just the ball going over the net. I walked to the bench and sat down. The sky was just the right color of pale blue, heralding a beautiful day ahead.

The shih tzu's owner was crouched down, throwing a rope toy for her dog. I worried briefly that Bingo would attempt to retrieve it, but he was busy on his trail.

"Oh! Great shot!" a woman yelled from the courts. Male laughter followed. I leaned back and peered through the hedge.

My eyebrows raised. It was the kid from Caleb James' room, the one he'd acted like I should have known.

What was he still doing here?

But what had me surprised was who the tennis player's partner was—the Amazon woman from room 418, Danielle.

Things seemed a little too coincidental to me.

"Isn't he wonderful?" The voice at my elbow made me start. I turned around to see the shih tzu's owner watching through the hedge, too.

"Oh? You know him?"

She stooped down to pick up her dog. I couldn't help but wince at the muddy paws against her shirt front, but she didn't seem to notice.

"Of course! Mark Everett! He's the Wimbledon up and coming contender. Pretty famous around here." She scratched her dog's head. "You can book a game with him if you want. He works for the hotel."

At that, my mouth dropped open. Of course. I knew the hotel had a recent contract with a local tennis instructor as a bonus for the guests. But, in the short time I'd been here, I hadn't made his acquaintance yet.

No wonder Caleb thought I was an idiot. I should know who comes and goes at the hotel.

Mark flew across the court continuing to throw out encouraging remarks. He was good. Very good.

I wondered who else he was teaching.

SIERRA WAS ATTENDING the front desk when I walked up about a half-hour later, looking just as cheerful as when I'd seen her yesterday. Her frown lines deepened when she saw me. But she wasn't what soured my mood.

It was the female officer standing in front of her.

"Detective Bentley!" I said, walking over with confident steps. "What's going on? Can I help you?"

She nodded quickly. "Hi, Ms. Swenson. Can we go someplace to talk privately?"

As we rounded the front desk, I murmured, "I'm sorry you were kept waiting. I had no idea you were here." I led her to my office and sat down across from her. "Would you like some coffee?"

She shook her head. "No coffee, thank you, Maisie. Don't worry, I just got here. The gal at the front desk was just about to call for you. Anyway, I have some good news and some bad news."

I swallowed. This sounded ominous. "I'm assuming this is about Mr. Olsen?"

She nodded. "I'll cut straight to the chase. The good news is that we've concluded our investigation of the pool and you're free to open it up today."

I raised my eyebrows. That was good news. "Lovely. Thank you for letting me know."

"I'm afraid that's not all. The bad news is that it most definitely was murder."

I took a deep breath. Finally, it was there. The elephant in the room that had kept rearing its head up again and again.

"How?" I breathed out slowly.

Kristi paused for a second and shrugged uncomfortably. "Okay, I'll tell you. But this is off the record."

"Yeah. You got it." I leaned forward, feeling breathless.

"The coroner is giving a tentative ruling cause of death as insulin shock."

Insulin? "He was a diabetic?"

Kristi shook her head. "No. But somebody injected him with enough to cause a coma ... and minutes later, death."

"Oh, my stars," I said slowly. I reached for a pen from the jar to give my hands something to do. Just fiddling with something relaxed me. "Have you been in contact with Mr. Phillips? How are you looking for the hotel to assist you with the investigation?"

"I'll be getting a subpoena for the guest list this weekend. Other than that, I'll let you know." She stood and held out her hand. "I appreciate both yours and the Oceanside Hotel's cooperation."

"Of course." I quickly shook it and followed her to the door. After our final goodbye, I pulled out my cell to call Mr. Phillips. It was a call I wasn't looking forward to.

By twelve, all the Comic-Con guests were gone, and the hotel held a quiet hush only broken by vacuum cleaners. I was antsy, feeling like I had a tentative hold on my job.

Mr. Phillips was not pleased, reacting much as I'd expected. What was unexpected was a text I'd received about ten minutes after my conversation with him.

—*Hope you'll forgive me. I stole your number from my brother. I wanted to let you know this is in no way your fault. I'll talk some sense into him when he calms down. Keep your chin up. This will work out.*

-Jake- the rational Phillips brother.

Well, that did make me smile. Sierra watched me suspiciously as I read the text so my smile must have been bigger than I realized. I quickly wiped it off and tucked the phone back in my pocket.

79

I headed to the computer to prepare the guest list for Detective Bentley. I assumed the subpoena would be there by the end of the day. I was about halfway through the list when my cell began vibrating.

"Ms. Swenson? It's Julie from housekeeping."

"Hi, Julie," I said, still scanning the list of names.

"Could ... could you come up to room 418 for a minute? I found something weird."

I paused and sat up straighter. Weird in the hotel business was a very fluid word. There were many, many things guests left behind, most too horrifying to go into detail here. So, it was with more than a bit of trepidation that I hurried up to the fourth floor to see what Julie had found.

The cleaning cart sat outside room 418's open door. I walked inside, looking around for the housekeeper. The room appeared empty.

"Hello?" I called. The beds were in the process of being stripped and looked like a bomb of cotton sheets had exploded.

"I'm in here!" Julie called from the bathroom.

I made a beeline toward her.

Julie squatted on her heels. She held out a fuchsia-colored makeup bag in her hand. "I found this under a pile of wet towels. There's medicine in it. She must have forgotten it."

She passed up the bag and stood next to me to watch me open it.

Inside the bag were several compacts, a tube of lip gloss, and random facial brushes. There was also a plastic pill bottle. I bit my lip before reaching in to snag it out. The label described sleep medication, prescribed to Danielle. The final item made my hand freeze.

It was a glucose monitor.

Kristi Bentley had said the coroner believed that Norman Olsen had been given an overdose of insulin.

"Now, follow me," Julie said, leading the way to the kitchenette. She opened the mini fridge and leaned back so that I could see inside. "Check it out," she pointed.

In the back of the shelf, there were several glass bottles of insulin. None were more than half empty. I pulled out the trash can from under the counter and checked inside. It held a small hypodermic needle with a cap sitting on top of tissues, a couple empty water bottles, and other garbage.

I found myself hesitating again, remembering Andy's face when Danielle spoke of Mr. Olsen. Would he have used her medication to poison him? It seemed too obvious and messy. And the trash had no empty vials in it. I shook the can. *Had house cleaning already emptied it previously?*

I carefully removed the trash bag and knotted it. Then I dialed Kristi. The call went straight to voicemail. I left a message. "Kristi, when you get a chance, I found something you might be interested in."

Turning to Julie, I said, "Let's leave this room as is until I can get hold of Detective Bentley. You did a great job letting me know." Julie flushed from the compliment and hurried out into the hall.

81

The cart's wheels squeaked as she rolled it to the next room. I took another quick glance around and then called down to the front desk.

The room had already been reserved, but Sierra moved the reservation to another room and marked this one down for service. She hung up on me afterward. I sighed as I shut the door. Just one more fire to put out.

CHAPTER 10

I headed to the office, deep in thought. I just couldn't wrap my mind around Andy murdering the man. He looked to be only eighteen, for crying out loud. Still, I remembered the flash of anger on his face when Danielle revealed he'd been fired.

Yeah, maybe there's a chance he would have gotten revenge.

Clarissa was at the front desk and gave me a sunny smile.

"Where's Sierra?" I asked.

"Lunch break. Hey, there's still fresh OJ left over from breakfast this morning. Want some?"

"Awesome, can you have someone bring me a glass?"

"Sure thing," she said, grabbing her phone to call down to the Breakfast Den, where the guests gathered every morning.

I walked into my office and sat in the chair. Kristi still had not answered my call, so I did the next best thing and texted Ruby.

She, of course, answered me back immediately. —*What's up?*

—*I think I found the murder weapon and can't get hold of your sister.*

The cursor blinked and then—*Give me two minutes.*

Ruby wasn't exaggerating. Two minutes later, on the dot, my phone rang.

"Detective Bentley here."

"Hi," I felt awkward at her intro. Do I call her Detective even on the phone instead of Kristi? "Listen, I found something you should come back down and see."

"What is it?"

"One of the guests who knew Mr. Olsen personally left behind her medicine. And among it was insulin."

"I'm on my way. Keep everyone out of the room." Kristi's voice was direct and no-nonsense.

———

DETECTIVE BENTLEY ARRIVED thirty minutes later carrying a small ice chest and, together, we trouped up to the fourth floor.

"Thanks for coming so quickly," I said.

"Thanks for calling." She flashed me a smile and pulled on a pair of gloves. As we walked in the room, her gaze darted around looking for anything suspicious.

"It's just over here," I said, walking to the fridge. She examined the sides of the fridge before squatting down to open it. After unclipping her flashlight, she shone it inside and then under the counter. Finally, she retrieved the insulin bottles and stowed them away in a Styrofoam ice chest.

I stood behind her, my hands clasped behind my back. "I'm surprised Danielle hasn't called to come get this. She must have noticed it was missing by now."

"Don't worry," Kristi said with a wry grin. "I'll be in touch with her soon."

"Over here is where I left the makeup bag and trash," I said, pointing to the bathroom counter.

Kristi looked over the fuchsia case before placing it in a plastic bag. She grabbed the trash and the ice chest. She glanced up, her gray eyes meeting mine. "You ever think about becoming a detective, Maisie? I think your talents are ill-used here."

I grinned. "I write murder mysteries."

Her face took a more interested expression than I liked at my comment. Somewhat abashed, I glanced down and clasped my hands behind my back again.

"Can I help you carry any of this?"

Kristi shook her head. "No, I've got it. I'll be in contact with her. Can you tell me more about the people that stayed here?"

"They're an interesting bunch. I was here earlier." We walked out into the hall, and I shut the door behind me. "But, before I forget, is this room free to reserve? You don't need it for anything else?"

The detective hefted the case against her chest. "I've gotten everything I've needed. But keep it out of the circuit for the next 24 hours just in case. I'll know more after I talk with the young lady."

"Now tell me," she continued as we walked down the hall. I punched the down button, and the doors immediately opened. "Why were you up here?"

I filled her in with the conversations that had taken place. As we walked off the elevator and up to the front desk, I finished the one-two punch Danielle had delivered about Andy being fired from Olsen Studios.

Sierra was back, her eyes on us.

Kristi frowned. "Can you get me his number, too?"

Mr. Phillips had already cleared me to hand out anything that was asked for by the police, so I walked to the computer, the other two not being booted up yet. Sierra sat on a stool in front of it and reluctantly moved as I stood waiting. She hovered over my shoulder, watching my every movement.

Irritation crawled up my back, but I ignored her. Now wasn't the time to say anything, not with Kristi standing right there. With a few keystrokes, I located his full name—Andy Davis—address, and phone number and scribbled them down. I passed the paper over the counter to the detective.

She took it and folded the paper, then slipped it into her pocket. "Okay, then. We'll be in touch." She gathered her stuff and headed out, making quick work of the revolving door.

"What are you doing? Creating scapegoats out of our guests?" Sierra asked.

"We found some evidence. Possibly even the murder weapon," I answered.

Sierra climbed back on the stool as if trying to exert some type of King of the Hill authority. "I heard it was the son who did it. This just keeps getting messier and messier."

What in the world? "How did you know Mr. Olsen had a son?"

She rolled her eyes. "Have you checked the news today?" Snapping the gum in her mouth, she turned the screen toward her and typed. The screen flashed with the local news.

"Caleb James to Inherit Father's Legacy."

Sierra turned back to me and said in a bored tone. "Isn't it obvious?"

My neck suddenly felt stiff and my fingers fidgety. I opened the drawer and pulled out a rubber band, instantly feeling soothed by something in my hands.

"Thanks for sharing. No, I hadn't seen that yet." I stretched the band and looked at her thoughtfully. "What's going on, Sierra? Is something bothering you at work or at home?"

Her eyes grew wary, and I saw her reach for her upper arm where the scar remained hidden. "What do you mean?"

"I mean you seem to have a problem with me," I snapped the band.

"I'm just doing *my job*." The vulnerable mask was replaced with a haughty look and her last words held a bite, a little dig toward her view of my job performance.

Okay, then. "Let me know if anyone needs me. I'm heading to lunch."

"I'm sure we can handle *anything* that comes up," she said with a sniff.

"Whether you think you can handle it or not, let me know if *anything* comes up." Without waiting for a response, I marched to my room.

CHAPTER 11

*R*uby called just as I poured myself a glass of sweet tea and was preparing to sit for lunch. Momma had made turkey sandwiches.

"Kristi get ahold of you?" she asked.

"Yes! Thank you so much."

"We haven't seen each other in forever. How about lunch?" she asked, this time her voice taking a wheedling tone. "Cafe Blanca?"

I needed to get away and glanced at my watch. "See you in fifteen." Honestly, I could use some girl-talk time. I missed my friend Lavina and our gossip brunches back in Tennessee. Those were some good times. But her best friend, Elise, had just moved back to town and I knew Lavina had her hands full. From what I saw, Elise seemed to get herself into the oddest of predicaments, not that I could talk after what I'd been through with this conference.

"Momma!" I called.

"What is it?" she answered from the living room. "I'm watching my stories!"

"I'm heading out. I'll eat the sandwich later." I wrapped it in plastic wrap and placed it in the fridge. "And don't give it to Bingo!"

"Pish!" came from the living room. Bingo peered around the corner after hearing his name. Seeing I didn't have food, he wandered away.

I grabbed my purse and headed to the cafe. The Florida weather was warm and humid, as usual. The sky was clear, but in Florida, so I had learned, that didn't mean much. Sun and a cool ocean breeze one minute, black clouds and thunder the next. And then it would clear right back up again.

The cafe was located just outside a popular tourist location—a paddle board rental business. Motifs of palm fronds and tropical flowers were painted on the outside of the building. Round wooden tables with simple, black, iron chairs were scattered in front on the patio, the tables spruced up with coconuts and miniature umbrella centerpieces.

Ruby waved to me from a table against the front window.

As I sat, a young waitress came over for my drink order. When she left, I turned to Ruby.

"Thank you for inviting me out. I think I'm overdue for a breather from the hotel. On top of everything else, Sierra, one of my receptionists, is giving me a hard time."

"Oh, girl! You poor thing!" Ruby gave me a sympathetic look.

"I just can't figure her out." I rubbed my forehead. "I usually always get along with everyone."

"Maybe she's just grumpy. Not everyone has to like you. Not everyone has taste." She winked as a laugh shot out of me. "By the way, Kristi just called before you got here. She told me to warn you to be on your best behavior and to leave the policing to the police."

I rolled my eyes. First Momma, and now Kristi? Besides, I was already too invested at that point. I felt like I had something to prove, both to Mr. Phillips and to Sierra.

My sweet tea was placed in front of me, and Ruby's was topped off by a smiley blonde waitress. Ruby ordered a grilled panini and, after thinking for a moment, I ordered one, too.

"I wish I could say I would listen ..." I said after the waitress left.

"But that's not the type of person you are? Oh girl, I can tell. Snoopy. Always so snoopy."

I couldn't help but laugh. "Is that so?"

"Of course. I mean, it takes a hard head to keep all the fancy pants in that place happy."

"That's definitely true." The tea was refreshing, and so was the company.

"Don't you remember when Douglas planned to TP the girl's camp? What did you do?"

I squinted, trying to remember back to summer camp. Seemed so long ago. I didn't want to confess I didn't recall it. That'd just give her permission to exaggerate the story however she wanted.

"Oh, yeah," I answered lamely.

"You snooped it out and ended up removing all the toilet paper from their dorms. And we had *chili* that night." Her voice raised in laughter. "Those boys were dying."

I chuckled. Those were some fun memories.

"And Fast Pitch!" she sighed. "Those were some good times." She examined her bicep. "I was in such great shape then."

I laughed. "Me, too. I wish I had the body now that I complained about back then."

"You and me both, girl!" Ruby's smile was mischievous. "So, not to change the subject, but who do you think did the deed?" She sipped through the straw, eyebrows raised in anticipation.

I looked up as the waitress brought us our food. "I don't know, honestly. There is so much going on with it all, some of it really gross."

"What's grosser than murder?"

"Well, Mr. Olsen may have been having flings with the young women that came to the Comic-Con. His son, Caleb, was labeled his biggest competitor on the internet, and today the story is that he'll inherit his dad's company. His wife is young—could be a motive there. And then I found out that one of his fired employees had access to the very drug that killed him."

"Wow, who knew there was so much drama in the world of gaming?"

"I agree. It's really shocking."

Ruby took a bite of her panini and chewed slowly. "Well, hopefully, they arrest someone soon."

"I hope so, too. We're having another convention this weekend, and the hotel is supposed to be packed again. I don't need rumors that we have a killer still running amok or people are going to cancel. Which means the hotel could lose some of the vendors." I sighed. "I could even get fired."

"Fired? How is this your fault?"

"Doesn't matter." I felt a wave of heaviness descend on me. I reached for my straw wrapper and twisted it around my finger. My eyes caught hers again. "So that's why I have to figure out what's going on."

She nodded, and we ate, the two of us people-watching as tourists came and went from the paddle board store. Soon our conversation steered back to memories of our summer camp days, and I felt some of the stress melting away.

"By the way," she said, holding up a French fry. "Have you met the hotel owner's brother?"

I felt my face heat as the memory of him wrapped in a towel came to mind.

She took one look at my face and let out a loud whoop. "I guess so, then!" She leaned over to whisper conspiratorially. "He's stunning, isn't he?"

I took a bite of my panini and let my waggling eyebrows answer for me.

Ruby laughed again. "And very, very single. The only trouble is that he doesn't seem to let anyone in after his engagement fell apart a few years back."

"How do you know so much about him?"

"Girl, no matter what the population number says, this is still a small-town at heart. All the gossip gets around. Anyway, I heard she broke his heart." Ruby sighed. "Too bad for the rest of us."

"Oh, I'm sure he'll find someone out there to mend his broken heart."

Ruby pointed a French fry at me. "And wouldn't you like to be the one!"

I shook my head. "Not so fast. Now you're sounding just like Momma."

"Well, I'm in good company then."

"We could all aspire to that, I suppose." I took the last sip of my tea and glanced at my watch. "That's all the time for me. Thanks for the invite." I slipped a twenty out of my purse and placed it under my plate.

"I'll call you later," Ruby called out after me. "And just so you know, his favorite color is blue!"

CHAPTER 12

*B*lue. I smiled as I walked into the hotel. Like I'd care about a thing like that. Still, the unbidden image of my blue summer dress came to mind. I *did* look awesome in that thing.

All right, knock it off. You've got a job to do, I admonished myself. Seeing Sierra at the front desk was like getting a cold bucket of water dashed over my happy feelings. I walked back to my office to see about the itinerary for the weekend's conference.

Once seated at my desk, I clicked open my messenger to check for messages. Five, ten, twenty ... I blinked as more messages came in. What in the world?

The top one was from Mr. Phillips. With a tiny whimper, I opened his first.

Ms. Swenson. What's this I hear about gossip flying around at the hotel? Something about you framing one of the guests? Call me ASAP.

The next message was from the housekeeper, Julie. *I heard the guest was the killer! Do I get some of the reward for finding him?*

I scrolled through the rest of the messages quickly—everyone from housekeepers to news reporters was questioning me about Andy Davis.

My mouth fell open as I pushed back from the desk. Frantic tickles started at the base of my neck, and I searched my desk for something, anything to hold. Finding a ball point pen, I began to click it on and off. *I've only been gone an hour? How does everyone know?*

Then, like a bell going off, I remembered Sierra's face. It was her, I know it was. I was so angry I wanted to break the pen, opting instead to throw it in the drawer as hard as I could.

Massaging my neck, I put a call in to Mr. Phillips.

"Hello?" he answered gruffly.

"Mr. Phillips, I'm not sure how you heard. The police only left with the evidence an hour ago. I didn't share this with anyone, other than the desk clerk, Sierra, who helped me look up his name in the system for the detective."

There was a long breath. "Sierra?"

"Yes, sir. That's the only other person that had the guest's name."

"Ms. Swenson, I'm sure you can imagine the type of negative PR that comes from having one of our guests the focus of a police witch hunt."

"Yes, sir."

"You're the one that alerted the police?"

"Yes sir, as soon as I was made aware of the medication left behind, I called the detective. I believe the case will be solved soon."

"What's the motive? The guest didn't like how the video game ended?"

"He was recently fired from Olsen Studios, sir."

A loud *hmmm* emanated from the other end of the phone. "All right. Thank you for getting back to me. It seems you really *do* have this under control. I'll be speaking with the desk clerk shortly. And don't talk to the press."

"Absolutely not, sir. Thank you."

The phone clicked off. I'd be lying if I said I didn't smile a teeny bit.

Okay. Back to business. I searched for the info on the next new convention. It was going to be a Fantasy/Sci-Fi multi-media workshop, with authors and filmmakers from around the country attending. Their request list seemed pretty simple and mostly focused around them being able to put up their sound system, chairs, and theater screens.

It was about twenty minutes after reading the workshop's itinerary that the medical bracelet popped into my mind. *For crying out loud!* In the rush of the other evening, I'd forgotten to put the bracelet in the lost and found. I rifled through a pile of post-it notes stuck to the side of my computer monitor to see if there had been anyone asking about it.

It has to be Danielle's. And I did see her at the tennis court.

But the tennis court was not directly accessible by the dog park. Which meant she would have had to be in the Park for Pups for some reason or another.

As I was puzzling this, there was a knock on my door.

It was Sierra, looking slightly mollified. "I'm here to apologize for allowing the news to slip about Andy Davis."

I thought of several different courses to respond, including a sarcastic remark about doing *her* job. Instead, I opted for something similar to an olive branch. "These things happen. I know how the gossip works at a hotel."

She nodded. "Clarissa's at the desk. I'm taking my break now."

"Fine. Hey, let me know if a guest comes looking for a medical bracelet."

"Whatever you say, *boss*."

I let her go without a response, not the most professional way to address her sarcastic last word, but my attention was caught. In my hand was a note that read, "Maintenance scheduled to enter Ms. Swenson's suite at one."

What in the world? Who scheduled that? Because it only could have come through me. I glanced at my watch and saw that it was after three-thirty pm. Frowning, I tucked the note away and headed out of the office and down to the suite.

Opening the door, the smells of chicken and vegetables greeted me from the kitchen. Despite the panini, my stomach rumbled in response.

"Momma, it smells delicious!"

"Well, darlin'," she answered from the kitchen. "If you'd just find yourself a man, you could quit working and have this every day!"

I kicked off my high heels and bent down to say hi to Bingo. "Why do I need to cook if I have you, Momma?" I whispered my answer to the dog. I'd never dare let Momma hear my sass. The animal's tail swung wildly back and forth as if agreeing with me, his pink tongue hanging out.

"So, what happened after I left?" I yelled. "I found a note that said you had maintenance come by? What happened?"

"Yes, I had to call. The maintenance man left just a little bit ago. And, boy, that man was an odd duck," Momma called back.

"Why?" I walked into the kitchen and climbed on one of the two bar stools.

Momma had her apron on and was cutting some carrots.

"What happened?" I asked.

"The power went out before I had a chance to fix my face." She sighed. "And, you know how I can't draw my eyebrows on correctly without the proper light."

I carefully checked Momma's face. Two penciled-on eyebrows raised back at my look. "Well, then, so he fixed it?" I reached over and snagged a carrot sliver.

"No. What's wrong with this young generation anyway? He was shaking like a leaf for one. He came in my room and just jiggled the mirror plug in the outlet a few times and then insisted on looking at the outlet in the bathroom."

"That's weird." The 'young generation' comment threw me. Both of the maintenance men were about my age.

"Well, he was a bit weird." Momma dumped the chopped carrots into a steaming pot. "He left without doing anything. About two minutes later, the power came back on." She shrugged. "Course, maybe the younger generation have a new way to fix it?" She gestured to the lights overhead. "As long as it worked, I'm not going to question it. He did ask weird questions, though."

"Questions?" I asked. Something wasn't right. The maintenance men tended to go about their business and stay out of everyone else's, making them some of my favorite employees in the hotel.

"He kept asking about where you were and what you did here. He wanted to know if you used to be a cop or anything like that. Very nosy for an electrician."

My blood turned to ice. "Did he do anything or take anything?"

"I mean, he fiddled with the outlet. It still didn't work when he was done."

I shook my head. "And then he went into the bathroom? Did you go with him?"

Momma nodded. "Do you think I'd let him back there to steal my jewels?" Her wrinkled hand raised to clasp the pearl necklace she always wore. "I watched him, but he didn't really do anything other than take the outlet cover off. Bingo didn't like him much, though. Did you, boy?"

Bingo gave her a big doggy grin. Momma reached into her pocket, pausing when she caught me watching. She pulled her empty hand out with a frown. "You shoo, now. I need to get back to dinner."

I nodded absently and then walked down to the bathroom. Everything seemed in place. Leaning down, I examined the outlet cover. *What in the world?* The plastic cover wasn't screwed in, and two tiny screws lay on the counter. I gave the face plate a push. It fell off into my hand. The hair on my neck raised. I didn't know enough about electricity to know if I was about to get electrocuted, but I could just imagine lightning shooting out of the hole. Why wasn't this put back together? Was the electrician planning on coming back?

Taking a deep breath, I peered into the hole. Nothing looked odd, at least nothing I noticed. As if I even knew what I was looking at.

Why would he want to check out this specific outlet?

I've got to call him. I searched for the maintenance number in my phone book and pressed send. As the phone rang, I idly looked at the plastic cover in my hand.

Every hair on my body stood up.

There was black writing inside as if written by a Sharpie.

"Lovely mother. Let's keep her that way."

I stood frozen, staring at the words before slowly hanging up. The first thought I had was, "Don't tell Momma. There's no need to worry her."

For the second time of the day, I scrolled for Kristi.

"Detective Bentley," she answered.

"Someone's been in my suite. And I think I've been threatened."

CHAPTER 13

*I*t was pretty anti-climactic when Kristi showed up. She snooped through the rooms, examined Momma's makeup mirror, bagged the outlet cover for evidence, and petted the dog. Bingo was in his height of glory at the attention.

Momma didn't question why the officer was there, still being busy making dinner.

I remembered the bracelet and pulled it from the pocket of my business jacket. "I found this the other night in the dog park. I meant to turn it in to the lost and found, but maybe it's another clue."

Kristi took the bracelet and scraped over the broken clasp with her thumbnail.

"Do you think it's Danielle's?" I asked.

She shook her head. "It looks like a man's. See the size of the bracelet?" She looped the ends together, making a circle that I could easily slip my hand in and out of. "Sometimes we get coincidences in this line of work." She handed it over. "Keep it safe and let me know if anyone comes looking for it."

I nodded and took it back.

"By the way," Kristi continued. "Miss Danielle also checked out about the medicine. She was shocked she'd forgotten it, and blames it on being scatter-brained from a date with the tennis instructor?" She lifted her eyebrows in question.

"I did see her with him that morning. I guess that could have happened."

"Well, she's still on our radar but you're free to open that room, now." She sighed. "You keep your doors locked and eyes peeled."

We said good bye and she left. I didn't tell her I'd talk with her soon. I didn't want to see her again for a long while, no offense to her. I needed some normal, no detective, non-murder, stress-free time.

I walked back into the kitchen where Momma had the oven open wide.

"Well, what did she have to say? Is she staying for dinner?" Momma asked, rearranging a pan in there.

"No, she had to get going. Anyway, I'm learning that the guy that died might not have been very nice," I said as I opened the fridge. I hung onto the door for a second just waiting for something yummy inside to jump out at me. *Mmm, there still were two slices of cheesecake left from the other night.*

"You get out of there!" Momma scolded, taking off her oven mitts. She set the timer and then walked to the kitchen table where a crossword puzzle book sat open. She grabbed a pencil. "Now what do you mean, died? I thought you said he was murdered."

"Yeah, murdered. I just don't like saying it."

"Well, the wife did it," Momma said, reaching for her reading glasses hanging from a chain around her neck and firmly pushing them on her nose.

"Momma!"

"I told you before, the wife is always the guilty one." She frowned at the paper. "And what's another word for quiet that's seven letters long?"

"Silence," I answered with a smile.

"Pish," she said. "I gave you a chestnut. Too easy."

"If it was so easy, then why did you ask me?"

Her laugh lines deepened as she looked at me. I could tell she felt clever. "It was a hint."

"Whatever," I laughed and headed to my room for my computer. "I'll give you silence then."

"I'm just kidding!" she called. Bingo started to get up to follow me until she whispered to him. I heard the familiar rustling of the cookie box and then the crunch as she passed down the treat.

"Those aren't good for him, you know!" I yelled from my door.

"What was that word again?" Momma sang back in a sassy tone.

Whatever. At my desk, I turned the computer on and brought up my mystery story. I was just getting to the part where the killer was going to befriend the store clerk. This was my world, a place I could escape the day's stress and make things happen the way that I wanted them to. I rubbed my hands together, grinning in delight at how creepy I planned to make it. I started typing.

Rain hit the window. The clerk glanced to see a pale face staring at her through the window. She suddenly wanted to run over and lock the door. But of course, that was silly.

"And, another thing," Momma called.

"What?" I said, trying not to sound aggravated. I didn't do well switching between my "reading/writing" hat to my "talking to other people" hat.

"We need more toilet paper!"

Toilet paper? We'd just bought some. "How are you going through a package of paper so fast?"

"I need the rolls for a craft," she announced. "I saw a delightful one on Pinterest. It'll be perfect for the Fourth of July!"

I whimpered. Lovely. Momma found more crafts on Pinterest.

CHAPTER 14

*W*ell, now I was thoroughly distracted. There was only so much I could take after knowing someone left a threat in my bathroom, and the news of Momma's creative Pinterest crafts had pushed me over the edge. I minimized my story and brought up the browser. *Time to see if there's any more news on Mr. Olsen.*

This time, I thought I'd try a different search engine to see if I got more results.

The first story that came up was about his death. The article called it suspicious, but they hadn't labeled it murder yet. They used the same picture I'd found earlier of him and his son, Caleb, with the sword. This article was more in-depth, with the headline reading, "Will Olsen Studios be Merged with Vertigo Games?"

The article was well written and stated that Caleb owned the company called Vertigo Games. It went on to further describe a friendly rivalry between the two companies. Apparently, Caleb had just branched out and created a one-in-a-million hit with his newest game *Madar's Forest*. I read further. It was a role-playing game that seemed to mimic and even mock a game that Olsen Studios had developed the previous year. It also was number five of the most popular games for the year.

Very interesting. So, the two men *were* rivals in a sense. I wondered why Caleb didn't have the same last name as his father. Out of curiosity, I typed in Caleb James.

First thing that came up was a link to Nova Southeastern University College. I clicked it and discovered the name Caleb James listed as an alumnus of the pharmacy program, graduating a few years earlier. His minor was in computer programming, which explained his career choice.

The next link showed his house address, his phone number, and people associated with him. I shook my head. It shouldn't be this easy to find information on people. I snorted at the next option. Apparently, for just a small fee, I could check his credit score, too. *And, what about his blood type?*

Among the stock articles was a seemingly unimportant link titled "Blankets and Sandwiches." I clicked on it and waited for it to load.

In the meantime, while I was distracted, Bingo had threaded his way under my desk. He was there now, all sprawled out and snoring. My feet were pinned against my office chair legs and were beginning to feel cramped and tingly.

"Hey, buddy," I whispered. "You want to scoot over just a tiny bit? Give me some room?"

As though it took every last bit of his effort, Bingo opened one eye. He wuffled air, making his lips flap, and then the eyelid dropped closed. Snoring, he seemed to sink even further into the carpet.

It was no use. I picked up my feet and sat cross-legged in my office chair. *Okay, so what's going on with this story?*

The picture that popped up was a black and white photo of a dirty man in a ragged coat. His feet were shod in old boots, and he sat propped against a building holding a sign. The sign read, *Vet. Please help.*

Beneath the picture, the article began.

James Place has already helped two thousand Veterans this year. Started by Norman Olsen, in honor of his war veteran brother, James Place offers a helping hand to homeless veterans to get them back on their feet. Run entirely on donations, the organization feeds, houses and helps wounded and homeless vets who have otherwise lived on the streets.

Norman says, "Some of them feel like they've given everything. And nothing's left for them. I'm here to show them that people care and respect them. Together, we can move forward."

Norman says the organization works as an advocate for vets, helping them obtain the physical and mental help they may need.

Named after his brother, LT. James L. Olsen, Norman hopes the organization will continue to help thousands more, and even expand into other cities.

I blinked after reading it. Wow. Maybe all my worries about Norman were unfounded. This man really was an enigma.

And Caleb... he must have taken his uncle's name as surname. Maybe to honor him? My brain was on overload. I could feel it starting in my temples, a pulsing pain that was getting stronger by the minute. Nothing for it. I needed Tylenol, dinner, and some sleep. I'd tackle the rest of this in the morning.

AT FIVE THE NEXT MORNING, I woke up to the throb of the headache. *Lovely*. Today was the first day of the Fantasy/Sci-Fi Convention. This one was being billed as the Sixth Annual Spielberg Tournament. The word 'annual' was a bit odd to me since the Oceanside Hotel had just begun hosting these, but I supposed they could have been held elsewhere. And the attendees didn't seem to mind the wording discrepancy, as was evidenced by nearly every room of the hotel being filled.

I dressed in a hurry and sidled out the front door so quietly that even Bingo wasn't disturbed. I checked twice to be sure the door was locked before heading down to the foyer.

Just like the last convention, even though it was six in the morning, the conference hall was already bustling with activity. Clarissa manned the front desk, so I walked into the hall to see how things were going.

Booths were in the final stages of being set up along both walls. A few men ran around placing chairs in rows. Covering the back wall of the hall was a movie-theater-sized projector screen. The energy in the room was contagious. Apparently, the convention was going to have a live show on the internet.

As the morning rolled along, the room began to fill with guests. It weighed heavily on my shoulders that this event had to go without a hitch. I truly believed my job depended on it. So, I spent a good bit of the morning introducing myself to the CEOs and heads of the production companies, or at least the people they had sent here to represent them.

This time, I'd hired a set of security guards just to monitor the activity. I wasn't taking any chances. I also had all other hotel employees, from maintenance men to housekeeping, staffing the convention. I caught one bellboy looking bored as he played on his cell, and walked over to him.

"How ya doing?" I asked.

He jumped and flushed with a guilty expression. "Sorry," he said, jamming the phone into his pocket.

"You're not into fantasy or science fiction? I thought this would be right up your alley?" I gestured to the front where several well-known authors sat on a panel. I suspected that they'd be answering questions after the movie ended.

"This stuff is too technical for me. DeadPool's more my style." He smirked. Then, as if thinking I'd disapprove of that answer, he stood straighter and clasped his hands behind his back. "But that's okay. I'm just here to make sure everything runs smoothly."

"Thank you ..." I double-checked his name tag, "Peter. We definitely want this one to go better than the last one."

He smiled. "No more dead people, right?"

My eyebrows lifted so high, it felt like they took my upper lip with them.

"Oh," he stumbled, catching my look. "I mean—uh—" he cleared his throat and then changed the subject. "I did see something kind of wonky earlier."

"Wonky?" Not a word I wanted to hear.

"Yeah. I told the security guy over there about it." Peter pointed to a guard by the front door.

"What did you see?"

"You know that guy that was here the day of the Comic-Con?"

"Peter, you're killing me here. There were hundreds of guys here that day. As well as monsters, aliens, and superheroes."

He wrinkled his nose and shifted uncomfortably. "It was the one you were talking with."

I nodded slowly, my impatience building. When nothing more was forthcoming, I prodded. "Yes? When exactly."

Peter sighed and bounced on his feet. "I don't know. It was out there." He gestured to the foyer. "At the desk. Anyway, I saw him in here again, today."

My eyelids fluttered closed. This was some of the most useless, possibly important, information that I could get. "Use some adjectives. Was he young? Old? Did he have horns?"

He opened his mouth to respond when I noticed a faint odor in the air. Acrid, like burning garbage or plastic. Glancing over to the sound booth, I saw smoke beginning to rise from a shiny black computer tower.

No!

No one else seemed to notice. On autopilot, I ran over to one of the emergency extinguishers on the wall and grabbed it. I yanked the pin out of the trigger as I raced back to the sound booth. The smoke had tripled by the time I made it back.

"Fire!" someone yelled out. There was a scream, followed by several more people yelling. People squeezed against me trying to see what was happening.

The sound booth was belching black smoke at this time. A large portion of the crowd bolted to the double doors, while a few were calling for the extinguishers. Someone screamed, "Call 911!"

A handful pulled out their cellphones and were recording the flames. I had to resist spraying them first as I pulled the trigger of the extinguisher.

"Hey, hey!" a man yelled, grabbing my arm.

I jerked away and ignored the protests as I directed the white cloud pouring from the extinguisher at the base of the flames, coating the computers.

Within moments, the flames were out. I dropped the extinguisher by my side, half in shock. *Did that just happen?*

The wall and computers testified that it did, with black scorch marks, as a heavy scent of burnt plastic and rubber hung in the air.

"What have you done? Do you know how much that system cost?" A short, slim man in a sports coat ran his hand over his head. He glared at the ruined mess.

"It was on fire!" I stared incredulously at him. "You're not serious?"

"That's thousands of dollars of machinery, not to mention the game that was on demo!" One hand yanked at his hair, his other skimmed over buttons on his cell phone's screen.

"Listen, I'm not letting the hotel burn down because you didn't want me to put out the fire!" I didn't even know why I argued with him.

Another young man with red hair stared at the mess on the table. He pulled at the bits and pieces of charred remnants. His brow furrowed as he lifted a ball of wires and metal pieces.

"Uh, Mitch," he addressed the man yelling at me. "What's this?" He held it up for the man in the sports coat to see.

"What the— Someone did this on purpose!" Mitch clasped the phone to his ear. "Hello? Police? Yeah, I'm at the Oceanside Hotel. Someone's intentionally set fire to my sound system down here at the Fantasy Convention. No, the fire's out. Ok, thank you."

"I don't understand ..." I mumbled as Gary arrived on the scene. He stood staring at the mess with his mouth hanging open, his face registering the realization that there wasn't much he could fix. Slowly, he shut his mouth and turned to me.

"Don't worry. I've got this." He patted my arm as he delivered what I suspected were comforting, but fake, platitudes.

The redheaded man spoke up again. "Someone made that with the intention of overheating the system so it would catch on fire. There's a 9-volt battery, exposed wire, and bits of charred paper. Somebody wanted this to burn." He set the offending ball on the table next to the deceased sound system.

I looked around the room. The guests were staring back at me as if expecting an answer.

"What is going on with this place?" Mitch glared at me.

"Hold on a moment, please." It was time to call the boss. Again.

CHAPTER 15

*M*r. Phillips answered on the first ring as if anticipating that something was going to be wrong. Good instincts, that man. "Hello?" His voice was tight.

"Good morning, sir." My voice felt like it matched his. "I'm sorry to bother you." *Just rip off the Band-Aid.* "There's been another incident."

"Incident?" If anything, the poor man's voice was higher.

"Yes, sir. A fire." I could hear him hyperventilating over the phone, not even able to get another word out. I continued quickly. "Don't worry, sir. The fire is out, and the police are on their way."

"Police?"

"I am assuming. Possibly the fire trucks as well, for a precaution."

"Why are the police on their way?"

This one would be a little harder for him to swallow. "It appears to be arson, Mr. Phillips."

There was no noise for a moment. I glanced at my cell phone to be sure we were still connected. Finally, he gasped, "I'll be right there."

He arrived in the same huddle as the police and fire chief. The fire captain inspected the ball of wires that the red-head had found and confirmed it was indeed arson. The police milled around and interviewed the guests in the convention hall.

My headache flared to epic proportions, and the light from the doors was making me squint. Mr. Phillips had just finished talking with a detective and was rapidly approaching me. I made my way around the desk and opened one of the drawers. After rummaging a bit, I came up with a paperclip. It would have to do. I began unbending the curves, even as I stood with my face held as professionally as possible for my boss.

"Ms. Swenson. It seems that I have your quick thinking to thank that there wasn't more damage."

I felt my eyebrows flicker. I definitely wasn't expecting that. Before my brain could process that I wasn't being fired, he continued.

"I can't imagine who would do something like this. The police will be reviewing the surveillance tape. I'm taking this personally." He frowned and rubbed his chin. "Maybe a competitor is trying to run me out of business?"

That was an angle I hadn't thought of. "I'm terribly sorry, sir. But I know the police will get to the bottom of this."

He nodded, still rubbing his chin wearily. I completely understood the feeling, since all I wanted to do was go to bed and pull the covers over my head.

"Thank you again," he mumbled. "I'm going to head out. This place is going to give me a heart attack." At the revolving door, he gave his parting shot. "Let me know if you hear anything at all."

I nodded before my attention was caught by another officer. Mr. Phillips was lucky he could leave. I had a feeling my day was just beginning. Plastering a smile on my face, I prepared myself for another interview. The paperclip was already straightened in my hands, now being twirled from one finger to another.

THE INTERVIEWS DIDN'T TAKE NEARLY AS long as I thought, and within an hour, the police had cleared out, and the convention was humming along nearly as well as it had before the fire. Stan McDaniels, the other maintenance guy, had rigged up another sound system, though not nearly as high quality as the original. But the guests seemed pleased as they sat in the darkened hall and watched a movie.

I glanced at my watch and addressed Clarissa, who'd just returned from a break. "I'm getting out of here for just a little bit."

"I don't blame you," she said sympathetically. "You gave us all breaks before taking one yourself even. Go have some time for yourself."

119

She was always so appreciative, and I gave her a quick hug. She was rapidly becoming one of my favorites. "You're seriously the best."

The contrast between Sierra and Clarissa was astonishing. What a difference an attitude made.

I headed out to the parking lot with the plan of running to Cafe Blanca to grab a panini. And maybe a sweet tea. I grabbed my keys out from my purse and thought about how my day had been and amended that order. Maybe a Long Island Iced Tea.

As I walked to my car, a flash of movement caught my eye. A man wearing a baseball cap was moving between the cars. Normally, that wouldn't have meant anything to me. But the way he kept his shoulders rounded and his face down struck my interest.

Like he wanted to hide.

A car drove beside me, cutting off my view of the baseball cap man. But I got a good glimpse of the driver.

It was the tennis coach, Mark Everett. The car slowed even more, and the man with the baseball cap looked up before jogging over. He gave me a brief sight of his face before he jumped into the passenger seat.

It was Caleb James.

I watched them drive away with an odd feeling. Why was Caleb here? Was this the man whom Peter had been referring to earlier? The one he'd tried to warn me about?

The car hit its turn signal at the hotel exit, waiting for the road to clear of traffic. I felt the idea building before I even gave it words. *What's the worst that can happen?* I jiggled my keys. *Yeah, right. The same thing that curiosity did to the cat.* I shivered, but still hurried over to my car and climbed in.

As I backed out, Mark's car had already reached the exit and turned right. The road was clear, and I was able to pull in behind them, trying to keep a good amount of distance between us. Another car turned right, and I allowed him to move into the gap between us. As he did, I breathed easier.

I continued to follow them for about ten minutes until I had a feeling about where we were headed. Moments later, I slowed down and watched him key the code to the Palisades gate. A minute later, I keyed in the code too, still miraculously remembering it from delivering the flowers a week earlier. I crept along the street, not exactly sure what I was going to do.

I was about a block away, when I watched the car pull up to Mr. Olsen's house. I coasted along slowly and then pulled over at the neighbors' house next to the curb. It wasn't a great plan, but what else could I do?

They didn't seem to notice me back there. Caleb jumped out and ran for the steps. As he reached the porch, the front door flew open, and Mrs. Olsen stepped out, wearing a pink sundress and looking as fresh as ever. She reached out and grabbed his arm as he started to pass her, smiling up at him. Then she continued down the walkway to Mark's car, leaving Caleb to enter the house.

Moments later, she was installed in the passenger seat, and the car drove down the street. I sat there, chills running up and down my arms, wondering what I should do. Should I continue to follow Mark?

Just as I was trying to decide, Caleb returned from the house. I ducked down in the seat and hoped he wouldn't think it was odd that there was a car parked out in the street. In this neighborhood, I probably stood out like a sore thumb.

Seconds passed and felt like an eternity. Not being able to see what was happening was driving me nuts. In a flash of inspiration, I dug my cell phone out of my purse and pressed, "record" and then lifted it just high enough it cleared the dash. Honestly, I was proud of myself for thinking of it.

I watched the screen. Caleb was a moving blur with something big and black in his hands. He walked to the side of the house and dumped it in the trash can. I swallowed hard as he looked in my direction, but he didn't seem alarmed. He walked over to a silver sports car parked in front of the garage and jumped in.

I let out the breath that I hadn't realized I'd been holding as he backed out of the driveway. He shifted his car into gear and raced off with a squeal of the tires.

I dropped the phone into the seat. My hands were shaking. *I must really think I'm Nancy Drew. Or some crazy person. What am I even doing here?*

I sat up and stretched my neck. *I'm someone who's desperate for my job, that's who.* Seeing that the hotel was attacked again, well, it didn't seem like the police were getting any closer to cracking the case. And here was the main suspect hanging around at the hotel right when there's an arson fire.

I distractedly nibbled on my bottom lip as I continued to stare at the house. Cautiously, I looked around—so far there hadn't been any curious neighbors examining my car—then pulled the key from the ignition.

What had he thrown in the trash? Was it possible it was a clue? What kinds of laws would I be breaking by checking it out?

I opened the door and stepped out, trying to shut it quietly behind me. All I knew was that it was worth the risk. I'd had two bad things happen in one week at the hotel, and my job wouldn't survive a third. I needed to figure out what was going on.

Taking a deep breath, I threw my shoulders back and stalked up the driveway like I belonged there. With as much confidence as I could muster, I walked over to the garbage can. The lid came off with a snap, revealing a black trash bag. Holding my breath, I ripped open the bag.

Inside was overflowing with wilting flowers. Lilies, baby's breath. White roses. I recognized the ones that I'd brought five days earlier.

I clicked the lid back on with a sickening weight in my stomach. *What in the world am I doing? What did I think I'd find?*

Slowly, I walked back to my car and climbed in. My head thumped back against the headrest. *This is ridiculous. Something is going on.* My head rolled to the right to examine the house again.

That's when I saw it.

Propped against the garage wall was a sign that had once stated "Olsen Manor." A black sword had been painted through the words, nearly obliterating them.

CHAPTER 16

I drove home with thoughts spinning crazily in my
head. It had to be Caleb. It had to be.

There was just one problem with my theory. I couldn't forget the
look of raw grief on his face when I went up to his hotel room
that morning. He'd looked broken-hearted. How was it possible
for anyone to fake that?

Or, was it grief over what he'd done?

I shot off a text to Kristi to let her know that Caleb had been at
the scene of a fire. It didn't make sense why he would have been
involved in the arson. What motive could he have had?

And what was going on with Mrs. Olsen and Mark, the tennis
instructor?

This whole thing was starting to feel like a slippery slope. I
wasn't so sure I wanted to step out on it.

I examined those questions, mulling each one over again and again. Truth be told, all those thoughts were helping me avoid the most important topic—the outlet cover. I shivered at the thought. My fingers twitched to hold something to comfort me.

Instead, I drove back to the hotel. The foyer was quiet when I entered. All the guests were still watching a movie. I peeked inside—something about green screen and animation.

Sierra was at the front desk, joy of joys. She ignored me, and I did likewise. Ever since Mr. Phillips had talked with her, she seemed to have her attitude in better check, for which I was grateful.

I scanned my computer for messages and then wearily headed back to my suite. The headache was driving out all motivation.

Just as I got to my door, my cell vibrated. It was from Kristi and simply said. —*On it.*

I assumed it meant that Caleb was firmly on their radar.

Inside the suite, I guessed Momma was in the living room. I could hear her show, someone was crying about being abandoned by their baby daddy.

I slipped off my shoes and walked into the living room, feeling like each foot weighed a hundred pounds.

Momma's back was to me in her wing chair, but Bingo sat up at my entrance. "Louisa May Marigold Swenson? Is that you?"

I smiled at the sound of my name. "It's me, Momma."

She struggled to turn in her chair. "You don't come sneaking in here like that. I'm liable to kung-fu you!" She made a chopping motion with her hand.

"You could probably do some damage." I sat on the floor and Bingo wandered over. Breathing deeply, I dug my fingers into his soft fur. "Hi, sweetheart," I whispered. He raised his nose and wuffled before pressing on my leg with one of his crocodile feet to keep me scratching his neck.

"Momma, I'm not sure I can figure it out," I muttered, not sure she'd hear me over her show.

She scrambled for her remote and pushed mute. "What are you gabbling about?"

I lay back on the floor. Bingo stood and walked closer until he was right over my face. He sniffed my cheek and then nudged me again with his paw. His neck dewlaps wobbled right before my eyes. I pulled him down and hugged him against me. Bingo responded with a wet lick on the cheek—which was a little more than I bargained for, but in the midst of this misery, I was grateful for the affection.

"Do you believe in me, Bingo?" I whispered to the dog. He rested his head against my chest and let out a nasally sigh.

There was a creak as Momma folded the leg rest back on her arm chair. "Maisie, I've always told you. You make hay when the sun shines, and leave the rest for the birds."

I chuckled lightly and draped my arm over my eyes.

"Now, you listen to me, Missy. Whether we stay in this hotel, or we live in a box, we're going to be okay. You've always worked hard, and you've always made me proud of you, girl. Whatever happens, happens."

I glanced over at her. "You'll still be proud of me if I lose this job?"

Her penciled-on eyebrows drew together. "Darlin', there ain't nothing you could do that I wouldn't be proud of you. I was tickled pink when you were born, and I guess I've been tickled ever since." She stood up, making Bingo alert. "Besides, I was born too early to be a hippy, but I always thought it'd be lovely to try. We could live on the beach and cook weenies over a bonfire." She held up a wrinkled finger and pointed at me as if I were somehow standing in the way of her dream of being homeless. "That would be fun, and heck, times a wasting!" With a smile, she stood up and shuffled into the kitchen, with Bingo jumping off of me to follow close at her heels. "But for tonight," she called. "I'm making pork chops."

"Just stay out of the microwave," I yelled back, with a grin to myself.

"Stupid microwave. That can't be good for your health anyway," I could hear her mutter. I counted to five, and before I'd reached it, there came the familiar ringing clatter of pans. "I'm fine!" she called to reassure me like she always did.

THAT NIGHT, I sat in my room with a full belly and a quiet house, determined to get some writing done. The conference had continued on throughout the day without a hitch, and all the guests seemed to be settled for the night. I glanced at the clock, just seconds before hitting one a.m.

The cursor blinked, a black line coming and going against the stark white of the screen. I was surrounded by mystery and intrigue, and yet it didn't seem to inspire me as much as I hoped. I knew the stress was to blame for a good bit of it. I was discovering that real life killers and your job and home being threatened kind of hampered the creative process.

I angled the table lamp to shine more over my notepad. Sighing, I took a few sips of my chamomile tea and reread my last few notes.

Protagonist is in the shower. Intruder breaks in and heads her way. He kills the electricity, and she is startled in the dark bathroom. She grabs for a towel ... There's a clatter...

I leaned back in the small chair and stared at the blinking cursor. My mind was still spinning in another direction, trying to connect the clues on Mr. Olsen's death. *Was it possible it was the widow? Was she having a love affair? The son? Or was it Andy, the ex-employee, or some other angry competitor I don't even know about?*

My pen bounced against my thumb as I thought. I looked at it, carefully moving it from one finger to the next, the gesture soothing me. Taking in a deep breath, I let it out slowly.

There was a creak in the floorboards in the other room. *Momma?* I tipped my head to listen. It didn't happen again. This hotel sometimes made funny noises at night.

Focus. Get back to the story. I sat straighter and poised my fingers over the keys. What about the insulin? And the medical bracelet still sitting next to the fruit bowl on my kitchen counter?

The sign with the weird sword drawn through it?

Nope. Nope. I'm not going to think about Mr. Olsen. I'll never get this book done.

I slowly started to type.

Feverishly. he stalked her. Miranda tried to get away. There was a flash in the air, and she threw her arm up and screamed.

I began to see my protagonist's character unfold as the comforting ticks of each letter popped up on the screen. My mind focused on the world I was creating. It was several minutes later before the odd noises outside my room finally broke the writer's spell. *There it is again.* My fingers froze. Was that the front door shutting? I glanced at the clock—1:30 a.m.

A creak made me turn my head. *Oh boy.* I knew I heard it this time. It was closer than before. Right outside my door. Every hair on my body prickled. I closed the laptop halfway and pointed the screen's light away from me. *Keep calm. Move quietly.*

The doorknob rattled. I blinked hard in complete disbelief. *Get a weapon. Move!* My heart galloped as I searched the desk. *Weapon...weapon?* All I saw was a Kleenex box and an empty teacup.

Why don't I keep more weapons around this place?

I stood unsteadily and tiptoed over in my slippers. Slowly, I walked to the side of the door, my inner voice cursing for not having at least a candlestick holder available.

And you call yourself a murder mystery writer! The inner voice hissed.

Shut up.

The doorknob twisted more, wiggling a bit as if checking to see if it was locked. I held my breath and grabbed my slipper off my foot, the only thing in sight. This was going to be a pitiful last stand.

Then, just like that, the doorknob stopped moving. I slid along against the wall and held the slipper over my head and waited. Nothing. I strained to hear, holding my breath. Was that shuffling? Footsteps moving away from my door?

Who could have gotten in here? Into my inner sanctuary? Past the security code at the front door?

I chewed my lip and waited, unwilling to release even a slipper when that's all I had to wallop someone with. After a minute, I pressed my ear to the door.

That's when I heard it.

Laughing.

The sound of male laughter faded away. There was a clack, sounding as if it came from the front door. My hand trembled as I grabbed the doorknob. Slowly, I turned it and opened the door a crack.

The light from the kitchen cast a lot of shadows but also illuminated the main rooms enough to see if anyone was there. The master suite door where Momma slept was opposite me. Her room still seemed dark. *Where was that dog?* Probably asleep on his bed next to Momma's.

There was a dull thump out of my line of sight, and a scream nearly ripped out of me. My pulse thundered in my ear and tension knotted my stomach. I pulled out my phone and pressed the button to activate the flashlight, took a deep breath, and finished yanking the door wide open. I flashed the beam toward where the sound had come from. The small, but bright, LED lit the kitchen.

The bracelet was missing off of my counter. And my front door was left open.

Turning, I raced across the hall to Momma's room. I flung it open, terrified at what I might see. My hand ran along the wall in search of the light switch.

"Momma?" I cried as I snapped it on.

Bingo lifted a lazy head off of the plush dog bed and blinked at me sleepily.

"What in tarnation is it?" Momma grumbled. She sat up, her hair wound tightly around pink sponge rollers. "Don't you know I need my beauty sleep?"

I jumped on the bed, making her squeal, and grabbed her in my arms. She didn't say anything, maybe feeling my heart thunder against my chest in both relief and fear. She patted my back, and after a moment stroked my hair from my face. I snuffled into her shoulder before looking at my phone. Quickly, I dialed 911 and summoned the police to the hotel for the third time in just over a week.

CHAPTER 17

"Yes, Mr. Phillips. I understand." The hotel owner's voice came through the phone with stern undertones. I held the cell slightly away from my ear, wanting to sink through the floor. Inside my suite, the police were canvassing the entire area in search of clues. I had Momma bunked in an empty hotel room two floors up, with Bingo by her side. Hopefully, she'd get more sleep. Ruby was also staying with her. I was terrified to leave her alone.

Kristi wasn't working tonight, and instead, I was surrounded by a sea of blue-uniformed, unfamiliar faces.

An officer walked up to me as I nervously paced the hallway with the phone.

"Sir," I said, interrupting Mr. Phillips, "The police want to speak with me right now."

"I'll wait," my boss grumbled.

I held the phone to my chest. "Yes?"

"I'm Officer Peterson. If you could just follow me for a moment," The officer directed, leading me back into the suite. "So, the only thing you've noticed that's missing is a medical bracelet?"

I swallowed and nodded.

"And it had been sitting right there." He pointed with his pad of paper to the kitchen counter.

I nodded again.

"And just when were you planning on turning over that piece of evidence?" he asked, his brows furrowed in disapproval.

"I actually did inform one of your detectives," I answered, a bit defensively. "It was determined that it most likely belonged to another guest since it was a man's size."

He let out a long, nasally exhale. "What did the bracelet say?"

"It said Diabetes—On Insulin. On the back were some numbers."

He nodded and wrote it down. "And you didn't hear anyone break in?"

I shook my head. "I heard a little bit of noise, but I thought it was the hotel creaking at night. Later, I heard someone leave. He was laughing."

"You're sure the laugh was a man's?"

I nodded again, the motion of my head throughout this interview making me feel like a puppet. *Just pull my strings to make me move* ... "It was very deep." A shiver ran up my back. "Sinister. I already shared all of this with your partner a few minutes ago."

"I'm just double-checking," he answered. "We're not seeing any evidence of a break in. Did either you or your mother lose your key card?"

"No." That wasn't good news. Only Momma and I had keys.

"How hard is it to program a key?"

"Not hard ..." my mind was whirling with possibilities. Could Mark Everett, the tennis instructor, have done it? Was he working with someone else?

"We're going to be spending some time interviewing the staff." He glanced around the room. "This place has been pretty popular lately."

"It's been crazy, that's what. And, I have someone you might want to look into." Quickly, I filled him in on my suspicions on Mark and Caleb, ending with, "Mark works here so it wouldn't be out of the normal to see him behind the front desk for some reason."

"Do you have some other place to stay?" he asked, this time his forehead wrinkled in concern.

"We're in another room now. I have it off the system, so no one knows where we're at."

He shut his notebook. "If you can think of anything else, please call us right away. Be cautious." He glanced over at his partners who were packing things up. "Looks like we're just about done here. Want me to walk you to your room?"

I shook my head. Somehow, I still felt safe, lulled by the daily repetition of walking the halls of the hotel. Maybe it was denial.

"You'd better get back to your phone call then," he gestured.

My eyebrows ratcheted up in surprise. I'd completely forgotten my call. Giving the officers a wave, I brought the cell to my ear. "Hello, Mr. Phillips?"

"Ms. Swenson?"

"Again, I am so sorry." My hand ran along the back of my neck. "I am horrified that all of this is happening."

He sighed. "You and me both. This is my dream hotel. Starting to feel more like Bates Motel these days."

"The police are getting to the bottom of this." My voice rose at the end of my sentence with a hopeful lilt.

"Kind of makes me wonder who that guy really was to cause such a ruckus," my boss mused.

I winced at the word *ruckus*. Despite everything that had happened, there still was a man whose life had been cruelly ended, and who had left behind family, friends, and a charity that did care about him. "Yes, sir."

"Well, go on to bed. Try and get some sleep. I'll be there tomorrow."

Lovely. As if the fire didn't feel hot enough already, my boss would be overseeing my work day.

"Yes, sir. Goodnight." I hung up.

The officers had left in the midst of my talk, with just Officer Peterson waiting by the door. "Everything okay?" he asked.

I nodded and followed him out as he shut my door.

AFTER A NIGHT of less than refreshing sleep, and with the day being already packed full, I wasn't sure a large mug of strong coffee would be enough. I even pondered how possible a straight IV of caffeine would be.

Momma had snored all night, but she'd never admit to it. She always blamed it on Bingo.

Speaking of Bingo, it was an extra-long walk down two hallways and an elevator, but he had his time with the dog park. I sent room service up with orange juice and toast for Momma while I scrounged the Breakfast Den for myself.

What I ended up with was a granola bar. I can't say what made me grab it because I'm more of a cream cheese and bagel kind of gal. It wasn't until after I unwrapped it that I remembered the bar sticking out of Mr. Olsen's mouth.

I crumpled it and threw it into the trash, wanting to vomit. Sierra eyed me with her nose in the air.

"Wasting food?" she asked.

I took a sip of coffee to wash down the queasy feeling. "I was just thinking about Mr. Olsen. And what he'd choked on." I fanned my face, suddenly feeling light-headed.

"Oh, that wasn't a granola bar that was stuck in his throat," she responded, shuffling papers. She didn't add any more, letting the silence build between us with her know-it-all air.

I gave up. "Okay, what was it?"

"It was a protein snack. Issued in about twenty-five percent of MREs." She filed the stack of papers in a drawer and set to fixing the pens in the marble pen jar.

"An MRE?"

"Meal, Ready-To-Eat. They use them in the military, but you can also get them over the counter. My dad used to take one with him whenever he went fishing."

"How do you know this?"

She shrugged. "I overheard one of the detectives talking about it the day they came through to investigate the pool."

I felt my forehead wrinkle. Something about this information stuck in my head as important. My frown quickly fell off as my face took on a professional look. Mr. Phillips and Jake, his brother, had entered the lobby.

"Looky, looky. Here comes cookie," Sierra whispered under her breath. She turned on her radiant smile. "Mr. Phillips and Mr. Phillips," she said, greeting them before me.

Not allowing her to stomp all over my authority, I walked up to meet them. "Good morning, Mr. Phillips. Sir."

My boss was dressed in a three-piece suit, his hair slicked down to the side. Jake was dressed slightly more casually in a business jacket and slacks, with an amused glint in his eye.

"Ms. Swenson," my boss said. He glanced around the lobby, noting the early morning checkouts arriving at the front desk. "How is everything going?"

"Everything's running smoothly, sir. Despite last night."

He raised an eyebrow as if doubting that statement.

Jake spoke up. "I heard about last night. How'd everything work out with the police? Did they keep you long?"

"No, they wrapped it up while I was still on the phone with Mr. Phillips."

"And how about you. Do you feel safe?" His eyes darkened sympathetically with those words.

I felt touched at his concern. "Yes, I'm doing okay."

"Mr. Phillips," Sierra interrupted. "I organized all the insurance papers from the fire yesterday."

Oh, my heavens. Was it only yesterday?

"Ah, thank you." Mr. Phillips walked over while I bit back a groan. Again, Jake's eyes took on a humorous glint.

"It's not your fault, you know," Jake said. "These things happen. One of the biggest reasons why I didn't want to be in the business. All sorts of crazy things happen at hotels." He raised his eyebrows to punctuate that thought and then strode forward to join his brother.

My phone vibrated then in the pocket next to my hip. I turned and peeked at the text as unobtrusively as possible.

It was a text from Ruby - *Join us for lunch at Applebacks?*

Who's us? I wondered, texting back. *Sounds great.*

CHAPTER 18

*a*pplebacks was busy with a colorful forest of tourists in Hawaiian floral shirts and kids wearing mouse-ear hats. I saw Ruby sitting with her sister in the back and headed over there. Ruby gave me a sympathetic look as I sank into the booth.

"Rough night?" she asked.

I tugged at the skin under my eyes to emphasize the bags.

"Well, I'm glad you could meet us," she said. Kristi was next to her and nodded in agreement.

"I'm glad you could come, too. I shouldn't be enabling you." Kristi sipped her iced tea, and she shook her head at me. "But I also can't deny that having someone who has access to all these people is beneficial to me in solving this case."

Ruby smiled at me. It was funny to see the differences between the sisters. Ruby was the laxer of the two, goofy and friendly. Kristi was more professional and serious.

"Technically, you aren't." Ruby pointed out, literally, with her finger swiveling between the two of us. "She's giving you information, and you're just playing the 'hot or cold' game."

"You know I'm game," I smiled. "I want this figured out as fast as you do. It affects my job, not to mention my safety. And even worse, my Momma's safety." My eyes started to burn, and I fought back the worry.

"Is it bad that I hope the murderer is there? I want to bring him down," Kristi banged her fist against the tabletop.

I cringed at Kristi's outburst, wanting the bad guys to be as far away as possible. "Yeah. I mean, I want him caught, too. I guess if he disappears, it could mean he'll never be apprehended for it." I held back my own suspicion that he wasn't that far away. Specifically, the Palisades.

"You sure you're not secretly an agent? 'Apprehended?'" Kristi smirked, arching a brow at me.

"Shh, it's a secret." Ruby laughed. "Secret Agent Maisie doesn't want anyone to know that she has ulterior motives for running around fetching special pastries for one guest or having another's clothing taken to a dry cleaner."

"She's really dedicated to her cover," Kristi chuckled.

"I wish that were the case." For a moment, I could almost dream. "Nah, I live out my detective dreams vicariously through my writing."

"Oh yeah! You're writing a mystery, right?" Ruby asked, sipping her Coke.

Kristi narrowed her eyes. "I forgot you'd mentioned that before. So, this stuff is more like homework?"

"I have to use it for some good," I murmured. I didn't like how they were looking at me.

"Does that sound as hard-hearted to you as it does me?" Ruby raised her eyebrows at her sister, who shrugged but made no response.

Something in my gut tightened. I had purposefully kept my writing quiet, and situations like this were one of many reasons why. Did they really think I enjoyed the murder? Yeah, it inspired me, but I had no intention of acknowledging that out loud.

"Oh, my stars. Maisie! We're just teasing you," Ruby said after looking at my face.

I relaxed and exhaled. "This whole thing is making me a little sensitive," I admitted.

"Of course," she reached over and patted my arm. "It's going to be okay. Isn't it, Kristi?"

Kristi grimly smiled. "I can tell you right now that we are getting very close."

The air suddenly felt electrified. *Close? Does she mean this is all going to end soon?* I hardly dared to hope.

"Here's some of what we have now." She held up a finger. "Completely off the record. If any of this leaks, I'll deny saying anything."

"Of course." I nodded.

The waitress came then, breaking the suspenseful tension. "Can I get you gals anything?"

"I'll take a Coke for me," I said. "And a chicken wrap."

The other two put their orders in.

As the waitress walked away, Kristi leaned in again. "We've narrowed down our suspect list."

"You've had a few?" I asked.

Kristi winked.

Ruby pushed her arm. "For crying out loud, Sis! Spill the tea already!"

"The widow Olsen's alibi has so far checked out." Kristi smiled wisely.

"What was her alibi?" I asked.

The waitress returned carrying a tray, and we sat up again. With a smile, she set down a frosted glass in front of me along with our plates of food.

"Ya'll think you need anything else?"

The three of us shook our heads. Ruby's mouth was already full.

"Okay, then. Ya'll holler if you need anything." She tucked the tray under her arm and headed away. Immediately, the three of us leaned in again.

"She was at the nail salon. The shop vouched for her, as well as her appointment time. The effects of the insulin would have been rather quick. So, unless she darted to the pool, stuck the victim, pushed him out into the water on a float, and then hurried back to the salon, she isn't the murderer. It doesn't rule out that she could have had someone else do it."

I nodded. That alibi seemed pretty solid. I bit into my chicken wrap. The barbecue sauce danced on my tongue, both sweet and spicy.

"And Norman Olsen definitely died of an insulin overdose," Kristi continued, picking at her food. She pulled a tomato out from her sandwich and placed it at the edge of her plate. Her nose wrinkled like she'd found a bug.

"Seems like there still could be a juicy storyline here. 'Lady hires the side guy to knock off the husband.' Clichéd, but could work." Ruby nodded to herself.

I took a long drink of my soda, considering that scenario. It didn't feel right to me, and not because it seemed like the easiest or most prominent answer.

"I don't know," I finally admitted. "It seems too obvious. Has anyone come forth with any gossip about her and another man?"

Kristi shook her head. "Not yet, but we're digging. We're going to crack somebody. And soon."

"And we would hear, right? The small-town thing?" My gaze flicked toward Ruby, who nodded. "Are there any other suspects?" I asked, dipping a fry in some ketchup.

Kristi spun her glass in front of her. "There are a plethora of former employees and current disgruntled employees, as well as other companies that he was either working with or working against. The man had a lot of friends, but he also had a lot of people who wanted him gone. Or at least ruined. But, so far, there are none that we're considering seriously."

"What about people running his booth?" Ruby butted in. "Any suspects there?"

I nodded, adding, "And, was there anyone close to him that was a diabetic?" I reached for my napkin, only to discover my hands had been fiddling with it on my lap. Embarrassed, I tried to flatten out the ball before wiping my mouth.

"We're still trying to find out. Unless they tell us, we need a warrant for that kind of medical information. Going through the list has been very time-consuming. One thing that we've found that's interesting—Caleb James went to pharmacy school."

"Interesting, how?" Ruby asked.

"Just trying to put all the pieces together," Kristi said mysteriously.

"Oh, for crying out loud." Ruby rolled her eyes when she saw Kristi wasn't going to be more forthcoming. She turned to me. "Is the convention going to be over soon?"

"Yeah," I answered. "Today's the last day. The big companies are going to do their presentations and job recruitment."

"Job recruitment?"

I nodded. "I actually think I'd have liked to have attended it. One of my favorite authors was there giving some advice. But, between the fire and a migraine, I was knocked out for the count."

Ruby made a sad face at me.

Kristi dipped another French fry. "Well, our hope is that by the time this convention wraps up, we'll have our case wrapped up too."

"How are you planning on doing that?" I asked. I glanced down. My napkin was balled up again. It was a lost cause.

"Time's running out for somebody. And there's only one person left without an alibi who was at the scene of the crime. The same person who had the most to gain," Kristi said.

"Who?" I asked. I didn't need to. I knew exactly who.

Caleb.

CHAPTER 19

*A*s I left the restaurant, something didn't sit right with me about Caleb being the main suspect. But, because I'd been so onboard with the idea before, this feeling took me by surprise.

I didn't understand why the police ruled out Andy Davis, the kid that got fired from Olsen Studios. And what about Mark Everett, the tennis coach? He spent a lot of time with Caleb.

I took the long way back to the hotel. I'll admit it; I really wanted to check out Mrs. Olsen's house one more time. The sign with the sword drawn through it kept spinning in my mind, and I wanted to see it again. Maybe take a picture of it this time. I could just kick myself for not doing it the last time I saw it. But, at the time, I was shaking from nerves and felt lucky just to get out of there without knocking down a mailbox or two.

Some Nancy Drew I was.

It wasn't long before the Palisades sign came into view. Gorgeous red Canna Lilies bloomed around it. Living this close to the ocean made me appreciate flowers even more. Not all plants could tolerate the soil, especially the closer you got to the salty water. I punched in the code and waited for the steel gates to swing open, breathing in the warm air. The day was gorgeous, and the sun shone in a clear, bluer-than-blue sky. We hadn't even hit the hottest part of the day yet. The temperature was 95 degrees and still rising at one p.m. Normally, I'd have the car's top down and a hat tied on my head. But since I was trying to do a bit of reconnaissance—emphasis on trying—I had on my darkest sunglasses instead.

My inner voice had scolded me on the entire drive. What on earth did I expect to find at the Olsen's? Maybe Caleb's car in the driveway? And how exactly would that be weird?

The neighborhood was just as quiet as the last few times I'd been there, so I hoped I'd continue to go unnoticed. *Hey, everyone, I'm a nobody, just a housekeeper going to work. Just a chef's assistant. A gardener. Not someone snooping around, I promise.*

I took my foot off the gas as I approached the Olsen house. There was a car in the driveway—several to be exact. I crept forward, peeking out the window at the side of the house. A groan slipped out, unintentionally, when I saw that the trash was gone, including the sign. Caleb's car wasn't in sight.

As I drove past the house, I caught a glimpse into the backyard. It was incredible—flowers, meticulously kept hedges, brilliantly green rolling lawn. But what else I saw nearly made me slam on my brakes.

In the center of a garden, straight out of a magazine, sat a private tennis court. Mrs. Olsen was out there wearing a short white skirt.

The one playing opposite her was Mark Everett.

My mouth dropped open. *I knew it! This is the second time I've caught them together. And he has access to making room keys, and the ability to roam the hotel unnoticed.*

Even more amazing, he wasn't even on the police's radar.

The two were focused on their game, so I stopped to watch. Mrs. Olsen swung and missed, then tipped her head back to laugh. Mark laughed too and called to her encouragingly. He sent a soft serve over the net. Mrs. Olsen's tan legs flashed as she raced for the serve and sent it back.

Not exactly like a grieving widow. Another thought struck me. What if Momma was right? What if Mrs. Olsen had been seeing the tennis coach all along? Was that enough motive to have killed her husband?

CHAPTER 20

$\mathcal{I}$ drove through the neighborhood and back out through the gate, feeling very unsatisfied. I needed some more internet time, this time maybe a thorough search on Mark Everett.

Momma wouldn't be home when I showed up. I knew she was spending time at the salon refreshing her strawberry blonde hair. I could hardly wait to hear the latest gossip from Genessa. I slid my new specially-made key into the lock, and the door clicked open. Bingo ran out of the kitchen with a guilty look on his face.

"Oh, my stars. What have you been into?"

He licked his chops and rolled over to expose his belly. *Great.* I wandered into the kitchen and looked over it carefully. Nothing seemed out of place. The floor was clean, dishes done, counters wiped. I glanced at the table. Just a chair pulled out, and the butter container left out.

Butter ...

I walked over to the table and glanced at the tub. The smears inside made it undeniable that Bingo had somehow managed to scramble up onto the chair and maybe even on the table. The butter had teeth marks and hair buried deep into the container.

"Bingo!" I exclaimed. Trying not to gag, I grabbed the container and tossed it into the garbage. *I guess that means I'll be spending even more time than usual in the Park for Pups.*

I wandered out into the hall to scold the basset hound. Bingo was nowhere to be found. *That dog is smart.* Finally, I located him in Momma's room. Not in his luxury fleece and cedar bed. No, the animal had managed to squeeze himself into the narrow space between Momma's king-sized bed and the night stand.

"Come on out, Bingo," I coaxed. The dog didn't move, but his tail thumped against the floor. "It's okay. I can't believe it isn't butter myself." I scratched his back with a smile. When he stubbornly stayed in the corner, I got up to leave. Poor thing was ashamed of himself.

Back in my room, I lifted the screen of my laptop. The battery was low, so I plugged it in and then went for a glass of sweet tea while the thing booted up. The carpet was soft against my bare feet. I brought my drink back and sat with a contented sigh at my desk. This was my true happy place.

My fingers flew over the keyboard and brought up a search engine. I typed in Mark Everett and took a sip of tea.

It was no surprise that the most recent news came up first, his place of employment at Oceanside Hotel. There was a tennis forum as the next choice. I clicked it and scrolled through mundane posts that he'd made about his thoughts on different tennis equipment. The white pages stated his address as twelve miles from the hotel.

There was an ad for his coaching services and another forum that reviewed tennis coaches. I clicked on that and saw he ranked pretty highly. Review after review praised him, and he seemed booked out for a while.

It was no wonder the Oceanside contracted with him.

Other than that, everything seemed pretty boring. I searched out colleges and saw that he'd graduated from the Nova Southeastern University College five years prior.

The news sent a zing of excitement through me.

That's the same one Caleb attended. Mark graduated a little bit earlier, but they'd been there at the same time.

But what does this mean? Just that they're long-time friends?

I staved off the growing frustration with another drink from my tea. Without even thinking about it, my hand wandered around the desk until it located a rubber band—one I always left there. I rolled it over my hand and onto my wrist like a bracelet, and ran a finger under it, spinning it.

I took a deep breath and slowly felt better.

Okay. Mrs. Olsen is next.

I typed in her name, and the search engine came up with a ridiculous number of Olsens. Backtracking, I searched out Norman Olsen and found his wife's first name.

Veronica. Huh. It was the first time I'd heard her name.

Google quickly gave me the down and dirty details. She was thirty-five—*my age, weird*—and had been married for ten years. That fit with all the family pictures I saw hanging on her wall.

But the next bit of information made me catch my breath. She worked as a clinical psychologist at James Place, having graduated with her degree from Harvard.

Wow, now that's a surprise.

I looked up James Place and searched for reviews.

Most of them were glowing. Apparently, Veronica Olsen was very respected in her field of work with PTSD. There were many accolades, and it started to warm my heart toward the widow. At the same time, I felt a wave of guilt for suspecting her.

Bingo decided at that moment to make his presence known. He poked his head into the entrance of my room.

I looked at him and said adamantly, "Good people can do bad things, too."

His tail gave two quick waves like he didn't believe it, but he'd humor me. Walking slowly, he came to the front of the desk and stood there. I moved my feet a tiny bit, and he took the invitation and slowly began to wedge himself under the desk. After turning a couple times, he'd successfully pushed my feet out of the way and up against the chair rungs again. He sank down with a satisfied sigh.

I giggled. That dog, I swear.

There was more to the story that had caught my eye, and I clicked it to check it out.

It was from a small-town newspaper located in the state of Ohio. The title screamed out boldly – "Local Man Blames Tycoon for Brother's Death."

The article read like one of Momma's stories. A military veteran identified as LT. Derik C. Smith was turned away from James Place. He was later found dead in an alley. The brother screamed injustice and attempted to sue James Place.

The brother had no chance. A small-town lawyer was no match against the fleet of attorneys and endless money that were in Norman Olsen's arsenal. The defense argued that the veteran had been belligerently drunk when he tried to enter James Place, and it was within the discretionary rights of James Place to turn him away in that condition.

The picture accompanying the news article was of the brother as he left the courtroom, hat pulled low. Despite his face being partially hidden, there was no mistaking the tear tracks and the angry snarl of his mouth.

I twirled the band again and took in a deep breath. *The poor man.* What a horrible story. My heart squeezed inside my chest.

"You ready for a walk?" I asked the dog. He might not be, but I needed some fresh air. I stood up and headed to the kitchen for his leash, Bingo following reluctantly behind me.

"Okay, buddy. Let's go." I snapped on the lead and opened the door. Together, we headed to the dog park.

Laughs and splashes came from the pool, making me smile. Things were finally getting back to normal around here.

My mind was busy with thoughts of military veterans, fired employees, insulin, and conspiracies. I understood why the investigation was focused on Caleb, but something wasn't making sense. Despite everything I'd read, I hadn't seen a hint of a familial fall-out. And I couldn't forget the way grief cut his face that day in the hotel.

I let Bingo off the leash to do his usual sniffing and slowly turned around. There was something more I needed to check.

CHAPTER 21

*W*histling, I called for Bingo. "Hey, sweetheart. Why don't you show me where you found the bracelet? Huh, buddy?"

He didn't veer from his scent trail, and I didn't have any food to bribe him. Sighing, I walked along the edges of the park, studying the area. *Bingo was somewhere around here, I think, when Jake called him.* Thinking about Jake made me smile.

Loud screams rose from the pool area, making me tense. The shrieks dissolved into laughter, and I continued on. The sun made me squint. I slid my sunglasses on and continued to scan the grass, hoping and praying it would turn into a clue.

It remained just ordinary grass.

Disappointed, I returned to the fence and walked along it, examining the bushes. My gaze caught something. What was that? Two broken branches at the top of the hedge were parted to reveal a bent top of the chain link fence.

"Someone hopped over and was caught," I murmured to Bingo. Turns out I was talking to myself since he was no where to be found. I glanced behind to see him chasing a butterfly.

"Some crime partner you are," I dryly muttered.

I stood up on my toes to examine the fence. The bend was sharp, as if caused by a sudden heavy weight. In fact, a small section of the chain link had disappeared. So, not only had the top of the fence been mangled, but a part of it had actually shorn off.

"I bet he was caught and dangled there from that bracelet. That must have hurt." I snapped a few pictures with my phone.

When had I last seen Andy Davis, Danielle, and Cynthia? I thought about it and realized none of them stood out as injured.

I gently pushed at the weeds growing around the base of the fence with my foot, searching for the missing piece.

A grin stretched across my face. There it was. A small glint in the dirt revealed itself to be the triangle top of the fence. I took another picture and then kneeled to dig through the branches. Dirt got under my nails as I pulled it out. I flipped it over in my hand.

Someone had really been stuck and needed some help to free himself. Or herself.

I sent the pictures to Kristi and whistled for Bingo again. This time, he came running over, all of his extra skin flapping away. I clicked on the leash, and we walked back to the suite, my brain whirling a million miles a minute.

THE REST OF THE DAY, I had to force myself to focus on work. The convention was closing down, but I still had a lot of work running back and forth for the VIPs.

Mr. Phillips showed up again, intermingling with the guests. I assumed he felt he needed to set minds at ease since the fire incident and do a little bit of damage control.

To be honest, when I saw who had accompanied him, the whole mystery nearly faded from the front of my mind completely. Jake Phillips was walking beside his brother as well, shaking just as many hands. I wasn't sure why he was here, but I couldn't help watching him moving about. Although I might have to credit it to my overactive imagination, I could swear his eyes met mine. Twice.

Inwardly I chastised myself. *Good Lord, woman. As if you don't have enough on your plate.*

I already had plenty of distractions with the real-world mysteries. The last thing I needed was a romantic infatuation, or more. Besides, being involved with the boss's brother could have some major drawbacks if things didn't go well. I glanced at his Rolex and—*My word! Are those real alligator?*— Harrys Of London shoes. *As if I even had a chance.* I snorted, immediately feeling heat in my cheeks at the sound.

I continued on with the evening, pointedly ignoring the brothers as they made their rounds. New guests checked in, even as the convention slowly dwindled.

Soon the front desk's phone was lighting up like a poor man's strobe light with requests from the guests. A vase of flowers to one room, a specialty wine to another, and on the list went.

Momma rolled in during all of the commotion. She stopped at the front desk and stared at me pointedly, even as I spoke on the phone trying to sort out two free tickets to the magic show that evening.

Her eyebrows arched with indignation when I failed to respond to her. "Yes, that would be great. We need the table near the front. With a complimentary wine." I spoke into the phone and held up my just-a-second finger.

Momma's eyes narrowed. I quickly put my index finger down before I lost it, instead opting for a thumbs-up and an overly-exaggerated enthusiastic face. "Nice hair!" I mouthed.

She smiled and patted her curls before sauntering down the hall to our room. Phew. That was one lady I didn't want to mess with.

Finally, the flow of guest traffic began to ebb as the majority of the guests had checked in for the evening, and were now out having some nightly fun. Our town was truly a trap for tourists, with its nightclubs, restaurants, singers and fireworks display. I didn't expect to see most of them until after midnight.

"You've got this?" I asked Clarissa, once again my right-hand man. Or woman in this case.

"Totally. Go have dinner."

I glanced in the convention hall as I rounded the front desk. It seemed the Phillips brothers had left, along with nearly everyone else, leaving the hall empty of mostly everything but chairs and litter. I shut the doors to the room with a mental note to make sure maintenance got on it in the morning.

Bone-weary, I walked back to our suite, not expecting dinner since Momma was gone so long.

My phone vibrated as I neared the room. Palming it, I quickly answered.

"Maisie?" It was Ruby.

"Yeah?"

"You'll never guess what just happened."

"What?"

"Go turn on the news right now. Caleb James just got arrested. It's on channel seven."

I keyed in the lock and ran inside, scarcely spending a moment to kick off my shoes.

"Maisie? Is that you?" Momma called from the kitchen.

"I'm busy, Momma. I'll be there in a minute."

"You hungry? I'll make you some of my famous cheesy noodles."

I smiled at the mention of a childhood favorite meal. Most people knew it as mac and cheese. "Sounds good, Momma."

I leaned over to switch on the TV, only wincing slightly at the sudden clatter of falling pots and pans. I guess a human could get used to just about anything.

Searching around Momma's arm chair, I located the remote. With surreal energy, I flipped through the channels and finally rested on channel seven.

The female reporter spoke in a solemn tone. Around her, a crowd of people swelled.

"We're here live waiting on the arrival of Caleb James, son of famed business mogul, Norman Olsen. Today, at approximately five p.m., a warrant was served on Mr. James for the murder of his father."

The Sheriff's unmarked vehicle pulled up, and an officer ushered Caleb out from the back seat. They'd thrown a sports coat over his hands as a nod to decorum, but anyone with eyes could see that he was handcuffed.

He looked up into the camera, and something in my heart broke. Caleb seemed to attempt to counter his emotions with stoicism, but he couldn't hide the pain and fear in his eyes.

I shook my head. That didn't look like the face of a killer. It looked like someone who had been framed. Maybe it was me being naive; I'd been accused of that before.

And, anyway, how did he get access to insulin? I shook my head. No, this was wrong, all wrong. But what could I do about it?

Police pushed back the crowd to make room for Caleb and the other officers. He was ushered into the jail, as the Sheriff took the make-shift podium to address the crowd. The Sheriff tapped the mic, and spoke in a voice that sounded like it had been created by chewing barbed wire, "I'm here to answer any questions."

Yells erupted around the area as reporters called for his attention. He glanced around until his gaze finally settled on one. "You. Over there. What's your question?"

"What do you think the motive was?"

"Mr. James owned a competing business with a likewise competing game. Other than that, it's for the prosecuting attorney to decide."

The shouts erupted around him again, interrupting one another in attempt to get the Sheriff's attention. The Sheriff looked and pointed again. "You."

"What was the murder weapon?"

"It's not being disclosed to the public at this time." His narrowed eyes darted around. "You," he chose again.

"Do you think he worked alone?"

"At this time, we believe so." There was a pause, and then, "You."

"How do you think this affects Olsen Studios?"

The Sheriff shrugged. "I have no idea. I'm not an economist." He glanced around one more time before saying. "At this time, I'm done answering questions. As the investigation proceeds, we'll continue giving updates to the public."

He turned and walked away into the jail as shouts and more questions followed him.

The reporter returned to the camera and gave her follow up. Frowning, I snapped off the TV.

Wrong. Wrong. Wrong. All wrong.

"Momma!" I called. "They arrested the man's son."

"Those dingbats," she hollered back. "Don't they know it's the wife?" She continued, and my mouth moved, echoing her next sentence, "It's always the wife."

I needed more information. I almost texted Ruby, or even Kristi Bentley herself, to see if one of them knew what was up. I hadn't seen Kristi on TV, but I remembered her mentioning at lunch that they'd planned to wrap the case up when the convention ended. What was she holding back on me?

What evidence did they have to arrest him? All I could think of was the motive—that hefty inheritance. How did he get hold of the insulin?

I closed my eyes and saw the replay of Caleb getting out of the Sheriff's car. That moment of horror on his face before he masked it. He didn't do this. I couldn't believe that. But who did? And how could I prove that I was right?

CHAPTER 22

J jetted a text to Kristi Bentley. —*Can you talk?* I knew I wouldn't be able to sleep tonight without some answers. How did I go from being a class A stalker of my own main suspect, to now defending him?

My phone vibrated from her response. —*I can play the hot or cold game again.*

Okay. At least a game I knew the rules to. —*Is the cause of death still insulin?*

—*Hot*

I wanted to ask how they thought Caleb injected his dad. My eyebrows furrowed, trying to think of how to frame it in essentially a yes or no question.

—*Is Caleb a diabetic?*

—*Cold.*

Hmm.

—But he had access to insulin?

—Hot.

How? Somehow with his pharmacist's degree? I had too many questions to play this game any longer, so I told her I'd talk to her later.

Just as Momma came through the doorway with the bowl of cheesy noodles, I remembered the top of the fence. Was Caleb the one who'd shorn it off?

———

THE NEXT MORNING, I wandered into the kitchen with a sigh. Momma was just flipping the last pancake onto a plate.

"You could have told me there was no butter," she stared at me accusingly as I climbed up on the stool.

"What?" I raised an eyebrow at Bingo, who slunk off under the table at the word "butter."

"Anyway, here it is." Momma slid the plate of pancakes across the counter. She drowned her plate in syrup and then passed the bottle over. After pouring two glasses of orange juice, she took her breakfast to the table and put on her reading glasses. With a concentration line forming between her eyebrows, she opened her crossword puzzle book.

"One thing I just don't get," I said, forking up a bite of pancake.

Momma set down the magazine with a sigh. She regarded me over the tops of her glasses.

"Don't mumble, Maisie. Just spit it out."

"What about the granola bar? What kind of statement was Caleb making with that? And why did he mess with our outlet, and break in later?"

"Who says that poor child messed with our outlet?" Momma frowned.

"Well," I was confused. "You said it was a young man ..."

"Pish. Age is different this side of seventy. Isn't Caleb the same age as the rest of those people at the whatchamacallit?"

"The Comic-Con. Yes."

"Those kids are practically babies. No. By young man, I was talking about someone in his mid-thirties. Your age. But, no one listens to me."

I shook my head, flabbergasted. "If you saw him again would you recognize him?"

"I may be old, but I'm not blind." Her magnified eyes blinked from behind her glass lenses. "I've seen him several times since."

Her response rocked my world. "What do you mean, you've seen him? Why didn't you tell me?"

"Why on earth would I tell you about an incompetent electrician?"

I closed my eyes then, remembering my decision not to tell Momma about the message inside the light switch.

"Although," she continued, looking back at her puzzle. "It's obvious he was only filling in for someone else."

"Why are you saying that?"

"Because he didn't know what to do. Young people these days. It's better he keeps to his own duties."

"Are you saying he works here?"

She stared at me like I had alien antennas. "Louisa May Marigold Swenson! What kind of a dingbat do you think I am to let anyone but an employee in my house?"

"I'm sorry, Momma," I said, scrambling off the stool. I ran over and kissed her, and danced away. "I'll be back in a little bit!"

"Where are you going? You didn't eat your breakfast!"

"I have places to be, and cases to solve," I hollered, searching for my heels.

"You aren't Nancy Drew!" were her parting remarks as I shut the front door behind me.

Smiling, nearly giddy with excitement, I ran to the front desk. This was the final nail in the coffin for Mark Everett. I could just feel it. He'd definitely be a fish out of water acting as an electrician.

The hotel lobby was empty, with the exception of Gary and Stan changing out one of the wall sconces.

"Hi, guys," I said as I passed by.

"Good morning, Ms Swenson," they shot back.

Clarissa was covering the front desk, reading her Kindle. She perked up when she saw me approach.

"Hi ya, boss! How are you doing?"

"I'm doing great! I think I can solve who murdered Mr. Olsen."

She set down the Kindle, still half-smiling. My enthusiasm must have been contagious. "What do you mean? I heard last night that they arrested his son."

"They have the wrong guy!" I leaned in closer to whisper. "I think it's someone who works here. But don't breathe a word." Clarissa shook her head.

Stepping back, I finished with, "I need you to call a staff meeting. Everyone who works here needs to be assembled in the conference room in an hour." I nearly rubbed my hands together with glee. I'd have Momma with me and she could subtly point him out. I frowned as the picture of her yelling and pointing flew through my head. We'd work on the subtlety.

Clarissa typed on the computer. "Well, I don't want to rain on your parade, but quite a few of the staff won't be in until three."

I thought about that. "Okay, put the word out that there's a meeting at three. Everyone who is normally off then still needs to attend."

Sierra popped her head out of the back room. "Everyone? I have an appointment at three-thirty."

Of course, Sierra would complain. "I'll make it quick," I assured her. She started to protest when I cut her off. "Everyone needs to be there. No exceptions."

She looked at me with a frown and shut the door hard.

Next was my text to Kristi. *I think I know who did it.*

—*Did what?*

I texted back—*Murdered Mr. Olsen*

—*We know who did it. He's in custody.*

I smiled with delight—*You have the wrong guy.*

—*What did I say about you playing detective?*

—*I can prove it.*

I knew it was going to drive her crazy. She quickly responded —*Who is it then?*

—*I don't know for sure, but I will by three. Can you be here then?*

There was a long pause. Finally, she wrote.—*I'll be there. But I'm not happy.*

I sent back—*Thank you!*

I felt super energized all morning. I couldn't wait until that afternoon when I had everyone assembled together, and Momma identified the man.

Sierra continued to give me the cold shoulder, cutting her eyes away whenever I approached. She obviously was very upset at the idea of missing her appointment. But, at least Clarissa was there, happily chatting about her hot date for this weekend and keeping me entertained as I worked on guest requests.

The front desk phone rang, and Clarissa answered. "Hello. Front Desk. Oh, I'm so sorry, sir. We'll get somebody right on it."

I glanced at her questioningly even as I finished inputting the requests on one of the VIP accounts. "What's happening?"

"That was Mr. McKnight," Clarissa said. "He's threatening to leave because his shower doesn't have hot water."

I groaned. That would be a problem. Mr. McKnight had specifically booked the room with the five-head shower spa.

"He wants someone to come up because he accidentally pulled the knob off trying to get it to work."

Guests, I swear. "Go grab Julie from housekeeping and make sure everything's okay. I'll get hold of maintenance."

Clarissa called for housekeeping to meet her outside the guest's room, and then alerted Mr. McKnight that she was on her way.

At that moment, Gary ran up, his forehead creased with worry.

"Ms. Swenson!" he called, breathless as he approached the desk.

One glance at his face and I could tell that it wasn't going to be good news.

"Ms. Swenson, someone's sabotaged the water heating system. We've been working on it for over an hour. I hate to say it, but we're going to have to turn the water off to fix it." He frowned at my expected response.

"Turn the water off?" This couldn't happen at a worse time. Half the guests would want to shower before they checked out. But what was I thinking? Who showers in cold water? "How fast can you guys fix it?" I asked

"About a half-hour. But some damage has been done. There's boxes that have gotten wet. Old decorations and event stuff. We don't know what you want to do with them."

Great. Water damaged décor, no hot water, screaming guests. Anything else? No, I shouldn't think like that. After the last two weekends, this would be a piece of cake.

"Sierra," I yelled toward the back room. "You're in charge for a few minutes." Then, waving Gary forward, I said, "Lead the way."

CHAPTER 23

*I*t was a long way through the hotel to reach the basement entrance. The hallway stretched before us. My gaze did the usual managery thing and studied the condition of the carpet and the cleanliness of the chair rail. I was surprised how far the basement was. I hadn't been down there yet, as there hadn't been a need.

He was quiet, shoulders hunched, coveralls faded over the knees. He plucked at the cuff of one shirt, and his work boots shuffled over the carpet.

We walked and walked, and turned down this one and that one, and finally took a brilliantly-lit set of stairs to level zero. The basement was still one more floor below down a private set of stairs.

"So, what's gotten wet? Table cloths and curtains?" I asked.

Gary shrugged. "Just says 'Decor' on the outside of the boxes. I don't know really. Stan's down there now trying to sort it out. We'll get it figured out. We just needed your input."

I nodded, but honestly was confused.

We marched down another hallway, this one painted a clean white. I knew it led to the storage for the kitchen and restaurant. The basement entrance was at the end.

"So you said something was sabotaged? How?" I asked.

His eyes widened. "Someone put a clamp on the steam outlet hose. It's just pure luck that we had the piece to fix it right here." He shook his head. "Seriously. What the heck is going on with this place? Murder? Fire? Now, this?"

"You've never had to deal with anything like this before?"

"No, I'm originally from Ohio. My old job was slow and boring compared to this."

We made it to the basement door, a cold slab of gray metal. He passed his key under the slot, and the light blinked green to open. With a grunt, he yanked it open, and we stared down the last set of stairs.

It was amazing how industrial and sterile the fluorescent lights made everything appear. Such a sharp contrast to the warm walls and carpets of the main hotel.

I shivered, thinking that someone had gone down there to be destructive.

"You ready?" he asked.

"What? Yeah. Of course I am." I slid my hand along the icy metal handrail for support. The steps were made of metal grating that clanged as we descended. I had to walk carefully not to jab the heels of my shoes through the sharp openings.

"Do you think I need to call the police?"

"The police? No. I think we've got this handled. Stan has an idea who did it."

"He does? Who is it, then?"

"He'll tell you when we get down there. He doesn't want to cause a huge drama session."

Drama? How could it be drama with telling me who broke the outlet hose? And how did that person get the key? "What do you mean?"

"I mean, I don't know the guy, so I don't want to get the name wrong. Just wait until Stan tells you."

A draft blew up the stairwell and sent shivers down my back. It tugged at my hair that had fallen loose from my bun. I tucked it back, surprised at how cold my hand had become.

Gary glanced back at me to see if I was following. "Just around the corner." His voice echoed in the basement chamber as he took the last step.

A scent rose, as I took the last steps. Dank, wet. A cross between fungus and rotten leaves.

My fingers twitched to squeeze something.

"Where is it?" I asked, wincing a bit at my own voice's echo. The hair on the back of my neck stood up.

"Like I said, right over there." He pointed. "Just look how wet it is."

I glanced at the floor, searching for signs of water. I could hear it, a drip against the cement floor. How could this be happening? Should I set up cameras down here to monitor this area? I know Gary fixed it but how bad was it?

"Aw, don't make that face. I'm sure the things in the boxes will probably dry out."

"How long has it been wet like this?"

"Not long, not long. We found it pretty quick. Like I said, the water mostly just got into the boxes. Some of them are filled with fabric stuff. We weren't sure what you wanted to do with them." He smiled at me reassuringly. "We'll get this taken care of, don't you worry."

His eyes softened and he gave me a nod. What was I thinking? Gary and Stan were the heroes. This would have been so much worse if he hadn't discovered the clamp. I needed to chill out. The last week had made me jumpy.

"Good job on finding it and fixing it."

We reached the storeroom door. He wrenched it open, and its hinges gave a metallic scream. He held it open, motioning me through. I understood it was gentleman-like, but walking into the darkened room was not something I wanted to do first. Something was off, I could feel it. My gaze dropped down to his arm that held the door.

His forearm displayed a large American flag tattoo. Underneath it was a banner that read, "Smith, Veteran, Friend, Brother."

My gaze flicked up to his eyes, which had tightened slightly.

"Come on," he said. "It's just right over there. Stan!" he called.

There was no Stan waiting. The room was empty, and the emptiness felt like it sucked the air right out of my lungs.

Flag. Veteran.

Brother.

I felt the pieces beginning to click together. I stepped back was already halfway turned around when he yanked me by my arm into the room. In an instant, he shoved me inside and the door had clicked shut.

CHAPTER 24

My eyes struggled to adjust in the dark. There was only dim light in the far corner, from a flickering EXIT sign.

I tried to pull away from his grip. Everything felt like it had been moving in slow motion from the moment I saw the tattoo. Smith was the name of the dead veteran. And what had been in Norman's mouth? That morning when he'd been murdered?

"MREs," I murmured. The word echoed in the dark.

My steps froze. He shoved into me with a grunt.

"You're too smart for your own good. You wouldn't leave it alone," he whispered.

"Gary, listen...." Why I thought I could reason with him, I didn't know. But I had to try. Slowly I turned to face him.

He didn't like that. "No, you listen." He grabbed my shoulder to try and spin me back. I launched my fist to claw his face. My foot slid in something wet. Mushy. And my blow glanced harmlessly off his collarbone.

"What do you think you're doing?" he laughed. "You think you're a tough guy?" This time he forced me to turn around.

I faced the darkness. I could feel his presence behind me. Despite my best efforts, I started to shake. "Gary, we can figure this out."

"Shh." He whispered. "Do you hear that?"

I couldn't hear much past my pulse thrumming in my ears.

He drew closer and I felt his breath against my cheek. Hot. Putrid. "Tell me if you can. Nothing's wrong. Listen for it and see if you can find the problem."

I swallowed hard and listened.

Nothing. And then a squabble in some unseen boxes and a sharp squeak of rat. My whole body trembled.

"That's right. Just listen."

My legs trembled so bad, my high heels rattled against the cement floor.

"What are you so worried about? I'm not going to hurt you. I just need some time to figure things out."

"Time. I can give you time."

"I need some quiet time. And you do too."

I heard his clothing rustle and then something cracked the back of my head. Instantly, I saw stars. My legs felt boneless as the floor rushed to meet my face. I barely had time to realize I was falling before blackness greeted me like a thief in the night.

And then there was quiet.

CHAPTER 25

*W*et. Cold. The chill from the concrete froze my cheek. Was I in a prison cell? Where was I?

I moved my lips, my teeth feeling loose. Carefully, I probed them and realized I was laying in a puddle of something wet. Was it water? Blood?

I blinked, trying to figure out how badly I was hurt. My head throbbed but the pain made me remember. He hit me! Had I been knocked out? How long had it been?

Where was he now?

Every muscle jerked. Adrenaline made me want to run.

Don't move. He might still be in here. He thinks you're not awake. I fought my urge to move and instead kept my breath even. *Listen. It's your only chance.*

I heard scraping over by the door. Was it the rat?

Then I heard him mumbling to himself. "I don't want to do this. I shouldn't do this. It's not your fault. I know it's not. But you made me. You forced me to do it. You wouldn't leave it alone. No. No. No."

Adrenaline flooded through me. My heart sped up in my chest, beating so hard I could feel it against the floor. *How long have I been in this room?* I could hear the hum of a pump, probably one of several water pumps down here. *Someone will come looking for me. They'll notice I'm missing.*

Then I thought about it. Stan wasn't really down here. Gary could undo his tampering with the hot water, and everything would be back to normal. Who knew I was down here? Sierra, right?

My heart squeezed when I realized she hadn't come out of the back room. I couldn't think of anyone who'd seen me leave with Gary.

My phone! Will my phone work? The concrete that bit into my cheek seemed to mock me. What was I thinking? I barely got cell service in an elevator. There was no possibility down here in this tomb.

"You did this to me." His pacing feet stopped next to my leg. I felt him nudge me with a shoe. "Wake up. You've had your quiet time. You're not dead. Yet."

Oh, I wanted to pretend. I didn't want to roll over and face him. Fear kept my breath coming in tight gasps.

"I said, get up!" his voice thundered in the empty room.

He knew I was awake. I didn't know what I did to give myself away. My one trump card, gone.

With a groan, I rolled over and tried to sit. Stars flashed around me. My face prickled from sweat as nausea grew. Roiling, my stomach heaved its contents, and I turned to vomit to one side.

He jumped back. "What's wrong with you?"

I swallowed and swallowed, trying to stop the heaving. Tried to breathe between the stomach clenching. Finally, it ended.

"It all comes back," he exclaimed. "You can't hide from what you've done."

I tried to look at him, but his face remained a darkened shadow. "I don't know what you mean."

"Your little meeting to gather everyone together. I heard you whispering to Clarissa. Ho boy. You just wouldn't let it be."

He paced again, making sure he avoided the puddle of vomit. "You should have left it alone. That whole family, all of them. They aren't nice people. Why would you help them?"

My pulse pounded in my ears and wasn't helping me concentrate.

Think, think, Maisie! Does he have a weapon?

I tried to remember what he'd been wearing. He was a maintenance guy. He had on a utility belt. There was probably a screwdriver attached, maybe even a box cutter. I thought about the chain link fence. Some kind of utility tool.

He hit me with something, but what?

He did hurt me. However, I was still alive. Was that proof he didn't really want to hurt me, or was it proof he was playing cat and mouse?

I needed to think. I had to outsmart him. I knew I could.

"I'm so sorry," he groaned.

I heard a thump and moved my head slowly, trying to see what he was doing.

He had slumped down to the ground and sat with his head in his hands and his elbows propped on his knees.

He continued to mumble. Back and forth between sorrow and anger. "Why? Why?"

"Gary," I whispered. And then a little louder. "Gary. It's going to be okay. We can figure this out."

He covered his face with his hands and screamed. Every nerve in my body fired and I bit back a scared scream myself. This man had lost his brother. He certainly obviously blamed Norman Olsen. But why come after me?

"Why are you doing this?" I tried to make my voice sound weaker than I felt. My head and heart drummed in unison. "Why are you trying to hurt me?"

He gasped, his face showing shock and fear.

"What did I ... what did I do to you?" I tried to force tears. I wanted to prove I was weak, even as my body geared to fight.

"You were going to mess it up! My brother was a hero! That man let him die. He sent him to his death. My brother wasn't drunk. He needed help, and they shoved him away. Well, I showed him. I showed him that he can't treat heroes like that."

I nodded, trying to create a rapport. "Your brother was Derik Smith?"

He looked down at his tattoo and rubbed it. "That man took my brother's life."

"Norman Olsen killed him?"

"He sent him away to die! It was the same thing! After promising he'd help all the veterans."

I nodded again. "I'm so sorry that happened."

"My brother's name will forever be remembered marred with a stain. Not the hero he really was. Not thought of with the respect he deserved."

"That's not right. He's still a hero. No matter what."

He licked his lip. "You think so, huh? That's not what the newspapers say. So, I brought shame to the Olsen name."

I was confused. Was he delusional? "I don't understand?"

"His son." The dim light caught the wild look in his eyes. "His son! Everyone will remember his son as being a back-stabbing loser who murdered his own father in cold blood. At least, that's how it's supposed to be. Olsen's wife and kid, living like royalty while my brother got tossed in the streets like garbage. I cared about my family. That scumbag ... he didn't understand family. After I killed him, I ripped off his wedding ring and ruined his son's life like he ruined mine."

It was starting to come together.

"How did you do it?" I asked glancing around. There were several red bricks scattered about, used to rebuild the crumbling areas of the basement and the boiler encasement.

He grinned then, a scary, toothy grin. The light made his teeth appear sharp. "Oh, you found something of mine. Didn't you? I had to take it back. My medical bracelet." He laughed, and I flinched. My movement made his laugh bellow louder.

I knew where I'd heard that before. In my apartment that night.

"I have a family," I whispered again. "My Momma. I'm here to take care of her."

His laughter pinched off, and he groaned again into his hands. "Why? Why? Why are you making me do this?"

As he sat crouched, his head hanging, I studied him carefully.

"I don't have to say anything. Nothing's changed," I said slowly. My only goal was to make sure he didn't hurt me.

"You say nothing's changed," he hissed. "Everything's changed."

"No," I said, drawing the word out low and soothing. "Nothing's changed. No one knows. Caleb is locked up. It's just you and me here."

"There's one too many in that equation," he said, his voice sharp.

Dear, God. Get me out of here!

I attempted to change the subject. "So, you have diabetes? It was your medical bracelet that had you hung up on the fence?" The memory was coming clearer of that day ... the noise at the pool fence. Gary showing up to help get the guests back into the building with his hands in his pockets.

"So, sloppy." He shook his head, raking his fingers through his hair. Sighing, he pushed up his long sleeve and looked at his wrist. There was enough light to see that it was bandaged. "I can

190

climb those things in my sleep, but I heard someone coming, so I rushed." His eyes narrowed as he studied me again. "It was you. Always destroying my plans. I tried to stop you with the fire. I thought that would be enough. Maybe get you fired. But no matter what I did, you were always snooping around. You just couldn't leave well enough alone, could you?"

Right near my foot was a broken chunk of brick. It was almost close enough for me to grab. Taking a deep breath in, I slowly shifted closer.

"Your plans aren't destroyed," I repeated again, this time more firmly. "It's going to be okay."

"It's never going to be okay." His body tensed.

We made eye contact then, and I saw it. He was watching me. Watching my every move.

My fingers twitched.

"Just what do you think you're going to do, sweetheart," he said, his lips turning up in a sneer. "Take me down?"

"I'm so sorry," I said. I lunged for the brick. He was moving, but not fast enough. My arm arched back, and then I flung it, just as if it were a fast-pitch baseball from all those years ago. I didn't need to hear the sound to know I'd connected.

He fell forward, as if boneless. I studied him for a moment, shocked at how unemotional I felt.

With a gust of fear, I scrambled to my feet, a little unsteady still from the blow to my head. But, I had more than enough adrenaline to propel me out that door.

I took the stairs with legs that felt like they weighed a thousand pounds each. At the top, I slammed the door shut.

With tears in my eyes, I leaned against the door, breathing heavily, I yanked my phone out of my pocket. The screen was cracked, but it was still working. I began to yell for help as I called the police.

CHAPTER 26

My screams for help brought a scared dish washer who'd been sent to the storeroom to bring up a fresh package of napkins.

"Hurry!" I yelled. "Call for security. Call for anyone! Someone just tried to kill me and I'm not sure how long he's going to stay knocked out."

Well, that kid darted off like a rabbit sprung from a trap. I was afraid I wouldn't see him again, but sure enough, he didn't let me down. It was only a few moments later when a whole crew of employees burst into the hallway.

The police showed up a little after that. Let me tell you, it was the longest passage of time in my life. Relief like I'd never felt before flooded through me at the sight of all those uniforms. They clattered down the basement stairs, guns drawn. I felt dizzy the entire time, not knowing what they'd find. What if Gary had escaped through the exit downstairs?

Fortunately, that wasn't to be. They found him right where I said he was, groggy and just coming to. The last I saw of Gary, he was strapped down to a stretcher and being hauled out to the service elevator to be taken to the hospital and then booked for murder.

Life was bizarre.

The next couple of days consisted of me cleaning up after the science fiction convention, the investigation, and spending time filling out reports for the police and the boss.

For the most part, everyone had been courteous. I had heard one person refer to me as a hero, and that didn't sit well. I felt for Gary Smith. It was obvious the man had some emotional distress, along with the difficult death of his brother.

At the moment, I was spending the last few hours of the afternoon out on our patio soaking up some sunshine. Sitting across from me was Ruby, who'd come over to try and help me recuperate with two new books and a new coffee mug. I looked at one now, a thriller I'd been wanting for a while now.

"How'd you know?" I asked, tapping the cover.

"Please. I know you. Speaking of books, how's yours coming along?" Ruby leaned back in the lawn chair. She hummed appreciatively as she took a sip from her glass. Momma had made fresh lemonade and cookies, happy to show off her skills. I knew she was expecting some praise from Ruby. She wasn't humble about showing off.

Momma didn't have to wait long. "These are excellent, Mrs. Swenson!" Ruby yelled, after biting into a chocolate macadamia nut cookie. Bingo raised his head from where he sat in the shade of her chair.

"It was nothing," Momma said, painting her nails at the kitchen table.

I scanned the blurb on the back of the book. "Well, I definitely got more than my share of real life experience. It turns out, mystery is a lot less fun in real life than on paper."

"I'd say smackin' a murderer upside the head with a brick and locking him in the basement is pretty awesome." Ruby bit her lip when she saw my face. "I mean, if it really happened to me, it'd be no fun."

"It all feels so surreal. I guess it's still sinking in," I answered.

"I just don't understand how you turned a boring hotel desk job into some kind of Agatha Christie novel," Momma called from the table. "I would have thought it was a simple and safe job, and yet here you are having to go all, I dunno, Jackie Chan on some crazy man."

"Jackie Chan, Momma?" I snorted.

"He's my hero." She came out, blowing on her nails. "But, he's still behind Davis Hamilton in my book, bless his heart. And don't be sassy, Missy. I'm pretty sure all those Jackie Chan movies I dragged you to are what gave you your hot moves."

I shook my head. "It wasn't that good of a move," I admitted, reluctantly.

Ruby sat forward and patted my bicep. "Fast pitch?"

I nodded, the memory of throwing the baseball during summer camp suddenly making me feel sick.

"It's over now," Ruby said to reassure me. "You did great. Caleb James is free, and justice was served. You can put all of it in your book!"

I shrugged. "I can't get over how broken Gary was about his brother."

"Well, sad or not, he shouldn't have killed someone," Momma said, waving her hand.

Momma always had a way with the obvious.

"I could never use it in my book. It's not right to benefit from someone's death."

"You're not benefiting from death, darlin'," Momma said. "You're benefiting from living through a deadly situation. That's different."

Sometimes I needed to hear her say those obvious things, just to make them sink in.

I smiled. "I suppose that's one way of looking at it."

"Now that everything is all behind you, are you going to check in with Jake Phillips? Or maybe I should say check out." Ruby winked at me.

"Please. That sounds like a mess and a half. There's no way I want to get mixed up with the boss's brother. I've seen the movies. Doesn't that always end badly? Besides, he barely knows I exist. No. I think, for now, I'll just focus on making it through this manager job safe and sound. Apparently, it takes more skills than I'd originally put down on the résumé."

"Ha! Whatever. You've always landed on your feet. And don't forget about that book." Ruby eyed me. "I've always wanted a famous author as my friend. Take me and your mom out on some fancy vacations."

"I like her," Momma interrupted. She smiled at Ruby. "She's classy."

I snorted.

Ruby asked, "How about that one girl? Sierra? Was she ever involved in this? Or was she just a jerk?"

I thought about her for a moment. Specifically, Sierra's scar came to mind. "I'm not sure what's going on with her. It feels like more than just sour grapes at losing the manager's position to me. Mr. Phillips put her on warning and, other than her fit about the meeting, she's been better." I grinned. "I'll get to the bottom of what's bothering her, don't you worry."

"Ha! Of course you will! Like I'd ever doubt it." Ruby grabbed her empty glass and stood up. "Well, I've got to get going. I'll bring this inside and see myself out."

I waved at her. "I'll see you soon."

"Lunch tomorrow at Applebacks," she said, pointing to me. Giving Momma a wave, she headed through the sliding glass door and closed it quietly behind her.

I leaned my face into the last rays of the late afternoon sunshine. I could still feel the chill from the concrete on my cheek. Like I said, life was bizarre.

But here I was. I'd made it. I was alive.

I had a second chance. And I wanted to do something with it. Even more than just living life, I wanted to find out what my passions really were. I owed it to myself to quit trying to look like everyone else, and figure out who I really was.

With my eyes closed, I listened to the faint splashing and laughter from the pool. A few birds trilled from the shrubs. Bingo snored contently under Momma's chair.

I breathed in deeply, filled with gratefulness to be alive. Grateful for my second chance.

"You ready to go in, Maisie, dear?" Momma asked.

I opened my eyes to see her gaze on me. I nodded and stood to walk over to her. As I grabbed her hand, she drew me down for a hug. Her arms were feather light. I breathed in the scent of her perfume, the same scent she'd worn when giving me a hug after I'd skinned my knee as a child. Tears pricked my eyes.

"Now, darlin'." She patted my back. "Life isn't so much about the smooth sailing, but what you do with the waves. And you did good, Maisie. I'm real proud of you."

I leaned back to look at Momma's hand in mine. A lump formed in my throat. Her hand, thin now, the back covered in a map of veins, gripped mine tightly as if searching for reassurance. I gently squeezed it back and hoped that reassurance was given.

I smiled as I remembered as she helped me as a little girl to walk along the top of a curb. I'd pretended it was a balance beam over hot lava, and she'd sworn she was wearing lava boots and was completely safe as she helped to steady me.

Those same hands hemmed my Wizard of Oz dress for a costume party, pressed over mine to help me knead dough, and fixed my hair for prom.

Momma. So precious and dear. She looked up at me now, her once brilliant green eyes slightly faded now, her cheeks still as pink as ever. And her hair, fluffed out in wild curls because she was due for another appointment at her "beauty parlor."

"Well, Missy," she said, patting mine. "What adventure does life have for us next? Because I can't wait to see what the future holds!"

The End

THANK you so much for reading Booked for Murder.

Follow Maisie in the next adventure—

Deadly Reservations.

Final Check Out

Fatal Vacancy

Suite Casualty

Check out the Flamingo Mysteries!

Mind Your Manors

A Dead Market

READ MORE about where Maisie came from in the Angel Lake Mysteries.

The Sweet Taste of Murder

The Bitter Taste of Deception

The Sour Taste of Suspicion

The Honeyed Taste of Betrayal

The Tempting Taste of Danger

Here is the Baker Street Cozy Mystery series! Free with Kindle Unlimited.

Cherry Pie or Die

Cookies and Scream

Crème Brûlée or Slay

Drizzle of Death

Slash in the Pan

My own personal story is shared in award winning Ghost No More, Metamorph Publishings winner of best Memoir.

AFTERWORD

Thank you again for reading Booked For Murder. The story continues with Deadly Reservation.

When Maisie Swenson stumbles onto the site of an ancient church steeped in pirate folklore, she's thrilled to explore it. She never expects to find a young woman lying in the churches yard clutching flowers like a real live Snow White. And just like the cartoon Snow White, this woman cannot be awakened.

As Maisie tries to puzzle through that situation, one of her guests is found in a coma, too. Only this one is mysteriously clutching a necklace.

Can she ever sort through all the crazy clues to find where the pirate and ghost stories end and a real life killer begins? Or are the folklore tales true after all?

"Awesome Book in this Series!"

"Kept me wondering who was the culprit and enjoyed the dialogue. She is a real person with real responsibilities and foibles. Good read."

"So good!"--Amazon reviewers

Made in the USA
Coppell, TX
26 October 2023

23394813R10118